The Trouble i

This produced a result that put the difficult hysteric's complaint in the shade for several hours. Sister, highly indignant at the state of affairs in Hunter Ward, marched into Sister Baker's room to hand out a first-class rocket to the suspected drug addict. She found Moll Wilson collapsed over the desk with her head resting on a sealed envelope addressed to 'The Coroner in charge of the inquest on Sister Hallet.' The erring nurse was deeply unconscious, barely breathing, with a feeble, but still recognisable, pulse.

From the ward below, Night Sister put emergency measures into action, and to this the lay staff responded at once with full co-operation. In fact most of those involved showed how thankful they were to work normally again for a spell.

But all to no purpose. The drugs Moll had secured with Mrs. Camplin's money, in her brief absence from the ward that night, were enough to kill six normal people. The hospital worked on her all the following day, but she died the next evening without recovering consciousness.

Other titles in the Walker British Mystery Series

Peter Alding • MURDER IS SUSPECTED
Peter Alding • RANSOM TOWN
Jeffrey Ashford • SLOW DOWN THE WORLD
Jeffrey Ashford • THREE LAYERS OF GUILT
Pierre Audemars • NOW DEAD IS ANY MAN
Marion Babson • DANGEROUS TO KNOW
Marion Babson • THE LORD MAYOR OF DEATH
Brian Ball • MONTENEGRIN GOLD
Josephine Bell • A QUESTION OF INHERITANCE
Josephine Bell • TREACHERY IN TYPE
Josephine Bell • VICTIM
W. J. Burley • DEATH IN WILLOW PATTERN
W. J. Burley • TO KILL A CAT
Desmond Cory • THE NIGHT HAWK
Desmond Cory • UNDERTOW
John Creasey • THE BARON AND THE UNFINISHED PORTRAIT
John Creasey • HELP FROM THE BARON
John Creasey • THE TOFF AND THE FALLEN ANGELS
John Creasey • TRAP THE BARON
June Drummond • FUNERAL URN
June Drummond • SLOWLY THE POISON
William Haggard • THE NOTCH ON THE KNIFE
William Haggard • THE POISON PEOPLE
William Haggard • TOO MANY ENEMIES
William Haggard • VISA TO LIMBO
William Haggard • YESTERDAY'S ENEMY
Simon Harvester • MOSCOW ROAD
Simon Harvester • ZION ROAD
J. G. Jeffreys • SUICIDE MOST FOUL
J. G. Jeffreys • A WICKED WAY TO DIE
J. G. Jeffreys • THE WILFUL LADY
Elizabeth Lemarchand • CHANGE FOR THE WORSE
Elizabeth Lemarchand • STEP IN THE DARK
Elizabeth Lemarchand • SUDDENLY WHILE GARDENING
Elizabeth Lemarchand • UNHAPPY RETURNS
Laurie Mantell • A MURDER OR THREE
John Sladek • BLACK AURA
John Sladek • INVISIBLE GREEN

JOSEPHINE
BELL

The Trouble in Hunter Ward

WALKER AND COMPANY · NEW YORK

All the characters and events portrayed in this story
are fictitious.

First published in the United States of America
in 1977 by the Walker Publishing Company, Inc.

This paperback edition first published in 1984.

ISBN: 0-8027-3051-5

Library of Congress Catalog Card Number: 76-53947

Printed in the United States of America

10 9 8 7 6 5 4 3 2 1

1

THE TROUBLE AT St. Edmunds Hospital had not actually begun when Miss Enid Hallet, retired ex-Sister Hallet, was admitted there to Hunter Ward.

St. Edmunds Hospital had been built in the first years of the century in green fields just outside the boundaries of south-east London; one of the Edward VII charitable outbursts, funds, offerings, in thanksgiving for the recovery of the monarch from an operation for acute appendicitis and to celebrate the new reign with new ideas. Particularly to meet the need for hospitals where convalescents as well as chronic or incurable cases from the big central London teaching hospitals could spend their days of recovery or decline in purer air and pleasantly rural surroundings.

St. Edmunds had, of course, been swallowed up by suburban expansion. By 1974 the Inner London Hospitals no longer sent their cases there; the medical staff was as provincial as in any large Midland town, and none the worse for that. From 1948 it had been administered by the Government through the National Health Service Regional Board, together with many other similar establishments, all competing for a share in the ludicrously meagre funds allowed them to keep the service going.

But the building had been well designed and built of good materials. Modern in 1903, it had been capable of taking, over the years, most of the expanding departments, X-ray, pathology, intensive care, and so on. The wards, by careful management and charitable private effort, had been curtain-cubicled, doing away with screens. Day rooms were added, television replaced or added to radio-with-earphones. Portable telephones, library books, children's toys, could be wheeled to the bedside. And on the top floor one of the general wards had, from the beginning of the N.H.S. era, been set aside for private patients and amenity cases.

At first Hunter Ward was known simply as the 'amenity ward'. Very ill patients, medical and surgical, were admitted there or transferred from another ward if their condition was such that the noise and bustle was likely to make them worse instead of better. Besides, there were thousands of Health Service patients who put themselves upon their doctor's panel because they could no longer, after the war, afford to be private patients. They had never been ill in public; they were elderly and would never swallow the social revolution. With luck, if they forswore their natural arrogance, they might secure an amenity bed. At the same time there were still plenty of moderately priced nursing homes about, though these soon faded away.

But a new generation of amenity patients developed; those who were insured nationally with their G.P.s but who also insured privately for possible operations or any other form of treatment that needed a consultant together with the complicated machinery for tests and treatment that could only be found in hospitals of one kind or another.

This group of patients was, as suffering people, just as worthy of a qualified consultant's care as any other. And so, in Hunter Ward, four of the beds were set aside for those who could afford, from insurance or otherwise, to pay the hospital for extra amenity and pay the doctor who attended them.

These four 'pay-beds' as they were always called at St. Edmunds, were not curtained but enclosed in thin board, with a door wide enough to take a trolley, opening on to the ward corridor. There were two of them on each side, while on each side beyond them, four curtained cubicles led to a bathroom and lavatory and a fire-escape exit to an outside metal staircase.

Outside the ward itself there were Sister's room and a waiting room for visitors, opposite these a kitchen, washroom with steriliser, store cupboard and another lavatory.

Though the trouble at St. Edmunds had not actually begun when the taxi bearing Miss Hallet arrived at the main entrance to the hospital, the driver was aware of it, for boastful rumours had been spread in the local pubs by the militants. As he carried Miss Hallet's bag up the steps, escorting her markedly uncertain progress, he said, "Know where you're for, love? I mean, ward and that?"

Miss Hallet stared at him. Having lived in a country village since her retirement and while there not exactly loved, but certainly respected, she said sharply, "Of course I know. I have been up for examination and tests, naturally, before being admitted."

The driver, feeling unjustly snubbed, handed her the luggage just inside the door. He did not attempt to warn her further, but waited to hear what would follow. Sister

Hallet, now on familiar ground and quite aware of the meaning of his words and of his action said "I paid you, didn't I? You need not wait. Thank you."

She moved off towards the pair of lifts just beyond the porter's glass-fronted lodge. She gave the occupant of this a brief nod as she passed, but did not speak.

Immediately she found her way barred by another uniformed porter. "Can I help you?" this man asked in a menacing voice that held little comfort.

Miss Hallet stared at him.

"I remember you, Wells," she said. "Perhaps you don't remember me. You were just starting at the front here when I retired. But you've noticed me coming here to see Mr. Campbell, four times over the last couple of months. So don't pretend you don't know Sister Hallet when you see her, even if I did show you how to behave in your young days."

During this long and harshly delivered speech Miss Hallet had walked round or beside the man until they reached the lifts, when she pressed the right button and waited.

Wells said, "I asked if I could help you. Do you know which ward you are going to? Can I see your admission card? We are not admitting private patients as from tomorrow, so —"

"*You* are not admitting!" Miss Hallet laughed. "What rubbish! I've a good mind to tell the governors right away! Who do you think you are, young Wells!"

His face had grown white with a very ugly expression. But the lift had arrived, its doors were open. Miss Hallet, handling her bag herself, stepped inside.

"I'm going to Hunter Ward," she said. "An amenity bed, for special Health Service patients. Never heard of them, I suppose?"

"The lifts won't be going higher than the third floor by next Monday," he said.

"Nonsense!" she answered in a ringing voice as the lift doors closed upon her.

The taxi driver, who had enjoyed the scene, was still standing inside the door and had now a broad grin on his face.

"Proper old vixen, eh mate?" he said admiringly. "Don't see many o' them about these days."

The porter made no answer but went back into his own part of the glass-fronted lodge to take out the blow to his pride on his unfortunate junior.

Meanwhile Miss Hallet had arrived at Hunter Ward. A young nurse saw her move out of the lift with a faltering step and ran forward to take her bag from her.

"I suppose Mr. Wells didn't send anyone up with you as it was for us?" she said.

"No," Miss Hallet answered. "Joe Wells seems to have developed a swelled head and a very strange idea of himself. He should be given notice at once."

"Come with me," the nurse said, moving into the ward corridor. "We have you booked for Bed 1. You look whacked. Let me help you."

"Call Sister," Miss Hallet said, following slowly.

Sister Baker was in her room. She was a good-looking woman in her middle thirties, brisk, efficient, knowledgeable. The surgeon in charge of Miss Hallet had already briefed both her and his registrar on the ex-sister's case.

"She won't be easy," he had warned them. "She was a brilliant nurse in her day and that was over sixty years ago. She could have been what they used to call 'Matron' of one of the great teaching hospitals, but her nature let her down. No one could stand her tongue, her bad temper, her slanders about staff, — all kinds of staff. She had to go, several times, I believe, for spreading slanderous rumours. She ended up here for her last ten years or so, perhaps longer. She buried herself in the country and had come back when she knew she was desperately ill."

"But you can't have known her here before she retired, Mr. Campbell," Sister said. She knew he could not be much over forty-five.

"Well, no. None of us three ever met her before, Sister. So much the better. But you'll have the worst of it, fending her off the other patients."

"What about me?" asked the registrar. He was at least ten years younger than his chief, a slim but well-built young man who had been a useful scrum-half in his teaching hospital rugger team.

"Always tell her the truth, Guy," Mr. Campbell answered. "I saw, the first time she came to my Out-patients, she knew far too much and had forgotten nothing. I think she's bound to be inoperable, but I propose to do a straightforward laparotomy to relieve this threatened obstruction if possible and set everyone's mind at rest. Right?"

That had been a week ago. A surgeon's turnover these days is very quick, though waiting lists for non-urgent operations are slow to clear. But Miss Hallet's case was genuinely urgent, considering her age and character and her past service. So Mr. Campbell was able to secure her an amenity bed, free of charge, within a week of explaining to her the results of all her tests and the conclusion he had come to.

As she undressed slowly, put on her clean nightdress and climbed into the warmed, comfortable bed, Sister Hallet remembered the long string of hospital beds, the thin mattresses, the freezing hard cotton sheets, one burning hot water bottle at the foot, the lumpy pillows, the open, draughty wards of those early days of her service — her lifetime of service. She held no rancour now, no sadness for the failure she had resented again and again, but never understood or accepted. She simply felt relief as she enjoyed her present comfort. Relief and a certain gratitude for this amenity bed. Not realising that her surgeon had denied her an ordinary ward bed for fear she would empty the ward of his more truly deserving patients or make some other havoc of which she was still capable.

When Nurse Shaw brought her a tray with tea and a biscuit she grunted her thanks, but did not smile.

"What's your name, nurse?" she asked.

"Patty," the girl answered. "Patty Shaw. The others on this ward are Moll Wilson and Tim Street."

"Why does Nurse Street have a man's name?"

Patty laughed.

"Because he *is* a man."

Sister Hallet grunted again. She'd heard of it. Not an orderly. Not a porter, like that insolent bully at the front door. A real nurse and called 'Nurse' into the bargain.

Patty Shaw disappeared beyond the curtains of the cubicle and Sister Hallet sipped her tea, beginning to feel a little restored and so able to meet the ordeal that lay before her. Not next morning, as she had hoped. No, Sister Baker had told her, a two-day preparation. One of her neighbours would be going to the theatre on the same list. Another of Mr. Campbell's patients in consultation with Dr. Fisher, Dr. Joan Fisher, a consultant physician and a woman. Well, that wasn't new; even in Miss Hallet's young days in the nursing profession there had been women doctors, but not many of them going for the higher degrees.

A gentle rustle at her curtains turned Sister Hallet's head in its direction. A gnarled hand was followed by a pleasantly rounded old face, with white curls above it and a substantial pink dressing gown below.

"May I come in?" Mrs. Mitchell asked, taking a welcome for granted. "Sister told me you had arrived and that she had rung up the hospital secretary's office to complain to him personally about your disgraceful reception."

"Come in," said Miss Hallet, flattered by this news. "A pretty pass, when the hall porter thinks he's a little Hitler!"

She pointed to the wicker armchair in the corner of the cubicle near the window. "Make yourself at home," she said, with condescension. "They gave you an amenity bed, too, did they?"

"No, not exactly," said Mrs. Mitchell, amused by the ex-nurse's manner. "No, I'm in for my annual complete check-up. My heart has been a trouble for six years now, but I provided for it long before that."

"Provided? Saw your own doctor, you mean?"

"Oh, yes. But insured, you know."

Miss Hallet stared at her. Who'd have thought it?

"Private patient, you mean? Pay-bed? What all the fuss is about?"

Mrs. Mitchell looked apologetic.

"Why not? I put my savings in it, from the shop. No children. Hubby died a year after we retired. I like peace and quiet. Had my fill of gossip in the shop all those years."

"I'm not against you," Miss Hallet said, beginning to find the old lady a bit of a bore. "I hope they don't refuse the ward service, that's all."

Her gloomy looks and harsh voice did nothing to comfort Mrs. Mitchell. Not like hospital nurses she'd known, she told herself. But caught back her criticism, because of course the newcomer was due for a serious operation and therefore deserving of every consideration.

She rose from her chair, slowly and with dignity, and paused by the curtain.

"I mustn't tire you," she said gently. "I don't think our doctors or the nurses will let us down. I'm sure they won't." Then she was gone and Sister Hallet pushed the bed table further from her, muttering, "Good riddance," under her breath and making the tea things on the tray rattle and bounce.

In the corridor outside her own private cubicle Mrs. Mitchell found Sister Baker checking a list in her hand. The nurse looked up as her pet patient reached a hand to her door.

"Now what have you been up to?" she asked, noting the faintly purplish flush on the old woman's cheeks. "Upsetting yourself again over young Lionel."

"Not this time," Mrs. Mitchell told her. "Only trying to make friends with our newcomer."

"Miss Hallet? And getting the brush-off if I'm not mistaken."

"Very much so. She sent me about my business in no uncertain manner. A most difficult patient to manage, that one, I should think."

"You can say that again," answered Sister Baker briskly, making her way up the ward, the list still open in her hand. Bed 3 was due for admission that day; Bed 3 was still empty. There had been no news of him the last time she had rung the front hall. Wells had not answered; the porter who did so just now had no information. If people were given the privilege of early admission to an amenity bed for a perfectly ordinary bronchitis it was up to them —

At that moment, below in the front hall, the chief porter was joined in furious battle, wholly verbal, but distinctly violent, with the missing patient.

"Here's my card. Can't you even read, dad? It says Hunter Ward, Amenity Bed 3, don't it?"

"And I'm telling you we aren't admitting cases to the pay-beds. Hunter Ward's closed."

"The hell it is! I've been given admission for today and I'm bloody well going to get it."

"You a union man, aren't you?"

"So what?"

"So don't you know private patients are against the principles of the N.H.S. Jumping the queue with their money —"

"Look, mate." The patient, now very red in the face, breathing noisily and coughing frequently, pointed a strong, thick forefinger at Mr. Wells and said slowly, but loudly, "You're unofficial, aren't you? Right. My union's paying for me, so I don't lose my job 'anging about waiting for a bloody bed. Right? So scarper! An' fast!"

As the pointing finger had now folded in among its fellows to present a very large, compact fist, the chief porter retreated a step or two. The patient turned and made for the lifts.

"It won't go up beyond the third floor," Mr. Wells shouted.

"If you've been muckin' about with it," the patient called back, peering into the passenger lift and running his hand over the indicator buttons, "I'll have some of my chaps in tomorrow to see it put right."

In the service lift beside him, the black porter said in his fruity voice, "You can come along of me mister. I go up to Hunter Ward just now."

Before Wells could intervene the patient had stepped in among the hampers and trolleys, the gates clanged to, and he rose out of sight.

2

Mrs. Zia Camplin lay back against her bank of pillows with a disagreeable expression twisting down the corners of her full lips. The rest of her face was hidden by a criss-cross of adhesive bandage, but her large dark eyes held the same message as her mouth, discontent now developing into anger.

She rang her bell, for the sixth time in five minutes. Sister Baker, who was sitting at her table in her room, sorting out reports for the consultants she expected to see very shortly, sighed and got up and went to her door. She was met immediately outside, by Trevor Leigh, one of the medical registrars.

"I didn't expect you so early," she said. "You must excuse me I have to...Nurse Shaw!" she called.

"Here, Sister," Patty called back from the open doorway of the ward bathroom. She was hauling out a very full laundry basket, overflowing with sheets.

"What on earth?" Sister began, as Trevor jumped forward to help the girl. "Surely they haven't —?"

"Oh, but they have," the registrar panted. He had pulled the basket outside the ward and parked it in the corridor near the lifts. "They're all in the kitchens having a union meeting with Mr. Bloody-dictator-Stalin-Wells addressing them. Dr. Thompson sent me up to tell you he'd be late, Sister. He's gone to find someone to work the lift."

The bell from Mrs. Camplin's room rang again and stayed ringing.

"I'd better see what she wants now," Sister said. "You helped her with her breakfast, I suppose, nurse?"

"Yes, Sister," Patty answered, not explaining that she had left the difficult private patient to get on with her second cup of coffee by herself. The woman had nothing the matter with her arms, for Christsake, only the cosmetic job in her Middle Eastern nose.

As Sister reached Mrs. Camplin's door Guy Harper, surgical registrar to Mr. Campbell, swung into the ward and checked at sight of her.

"Ah! Mr. Harper. Providential!" Sister exclaimed. "I dreaded being bogged down here." She moved her head in the direction of Mrs. Camplin's door. "Is Mr. Campbell coming up?"

"Well, yes," the young man answered. "But it's to see the shipping chap he's doing tomorrow morning, principally...Then..."

"Mr. Graham? That'll be good news for him. He's due to sail in a fortnight."

"I know. But Mrs. Camplin won't be seeing Mr. Turner before tomorrow."

"I wish you'd go in and soothe her. She's raising hell this morning according to Nurse Shaw. Tell her we're doing our best, but she'll be lucky if she gets any lunch at all unless she pipes down and stops bothering my nurses every five minutes."

"I'll be delighted," said Guy, opening Mrs. Camplin's

door so suddenly and bouncing in so breezily that the patient dropped the bell push over the side of the bed and he was able to kick the flex beyond her reach.

He settled down to explain to her how the present situation about private or pay-beds in N.H.S. hospitals had developed from a few ignorant growls about unfairness to a full scale refusal of any work at all on behalf of a small number of unfortunate sufferers.

"In my country," said Mrs. Camplin darkly, "we should arrest these strikers and cut off their right hands."

"Not a bad idea," said Guy cheerfully. "Quite a few only do one hand's turn as it is."

But there was so much contempt in his grey eyes behind the flippancy of his remark that it silenced Mrs. Camplin for a moment. But only for a moment. Her anger flared again.

"I pay for service," she proclaimed. "I pay very much money and now there is no service. I demand service. I will not be cheated! I —"

"You shall have service," said Ian Campbell's crisp Scottish voice behind Harper's back. The registrar swung round and stepped back from the bed.

"Mrs. Camplin," said Campbell, "Mr. Turner is sending in a special nurse for you at once, to deal with the present emergency. He wants me to change your dressings after the nurse gets here and he will come himself tomorrow, as arranged. All right?"

Mrs. Camplin relaxed. Her surgeon had taken her case in hand with immediate serious concern. The British were wonderful, especially in a crisis. Some people said that was a myth, but it was not so. It was true. She sank back on her pillows. She allowed her full lips and her lustrous eyes to smile at Mr. Campbell.

The two men left the room, Guy Harper kicking the flex of the bell push a little further from the patient's hand.

They found Sister Baker talking to a stranger who had that moment arrived and was taking off her uniform coat and beret. It was the agency nurse, middle-aged, tall, her face lined and burnt by years spent in hot, dry climates.

Mr. Campbell shook hands with her and spoke a few words about Mrs. Camplin with a warning hint of character trouble.

The nurse laughed.

"I've been freelance for years, sir," she said. "Mostly east of Suez. I can give her Arabic, Persian, two Turkish dialects or what have you, if she'd like it."

"She'd ring your neck if you gave her anything but the Queen's Oxford English," said Campbell.

He turned to Harper.

"That'll have cooked the Camplin's goose," he said as Sister went off with Nurse Biggs. "Come on. We've got to make up our minds about Miss Parker. Hysteria plus. But a grumbling appendix for sure. To operate or not to operate. I'd like to put her on the list for tomorrow. Then I'd have my list all from here and organise it with the theatre and the lifts to defeat Wells's nonsense."

"Graham, hernia. Parker appendix. Hallet?"

"Laparotomy. I told you when we spoke to Sister about her. Probably malignant. Possibly inoperable. Come along with me now and see that jittery girl. Then you'd better change Miss Adams's dressings. Leave them all off if possible. She should be fit to go in a couple of days from now."

Miss Daphne Parker had been given a bed in cubicle 2, next to Sister Hallet. She had been moved up to

Hunter Ward because her inborn shyness and nervousness had been so much increased by the experience of an open ward for women, that diagnosis of her true condition had been impossible. The consultant physician, Dr. Joan Fisher, feeling utterly baffled, had called in Mr. Campbell. He had fared no better. When he laid a gentle, exploring hand on her painfully thin abdomen, she had shrieked and flung herself away from him. Without a word he had left the ward to telephone and came back quickly.

"You are too upset at present," he told Miss Parker, "for me to examine you at all. I am having you moved to Hunter Ward where you will be in a cubicle to yourself and can settle down. Dr. Fisher thinks your appendix may be the cause of your illness. When I am able to examine you I'll tell you if I agree."

"An operation?" Miss Parker gasped, but it was clear that the prospect did not appal her. On the contrary her eyes brightened.

"Perhaps."

"But that's the private ward, doctor. I couldn't afford..."

'Mr. Campbell frowned.

"It is not. It is where private patients go, but the beds are for anyone who needs them, any Health Service patient, at a small charge for keep. No fee for treatment. Certainly none if you can't afford it."

"Then why...?"

But Mr. Campbell had left her and with Dr. Fisher beside him was walking away.

That had been two days ago. Now, with Guy Harper joining them, Mr. Campbell made up his mind to operate. The girl had made no fuss at all when he examined her. She had only said, in a small, shaky voice, "Will I have to wait long, doctor?"

"No," Campbell had told her. "Tomorrow morning, Guy? Can we squeeze her in?"

"Sure."

That had been window dressing, since he and the registrar had already fixed it provisionally. In the corridor outside cubicle 2, Guy got out his list and underlined Parker, appendix.

It was a dull list apart from Miss Hallet, and short, but that was on account of the state of chaos. Perhaps there was an off chance he might get the hernia to do himself, except it was a real private patient. Oh, hell! Damn Joe Wells.

At a nod from the surgeon he went away to fetch a nurse and a trolley for cubicle 4, next but one to Miss Parker, where a school teacher was recovering from cuts and bruises to her face, given her by an over-ripe pupil, whose long hair and infant beard upheld his plea that he was too old for school at sixteen and would bloody show them, her included.

The nurses, however, were rushing about in a state of confusion because both the lifts and the telephone were now silent, the dirty linen piled up in the corridor and Sister away downstairs to find out when the promised voluntary help for meals was likely to arrive.

Nurse Patty Shaw did however manage to secure a trolley for Guy with dressings and pushed it up the passage between the cubicles and inside the curtains of Bed 4.

"Can't stop," she said ruefully, for helping Guy Harper had become a looked-for treat in her day. "Why can't you have Assad Ali?"

"Mr. Assad," corrected Guy, to tease her. "Because

he's got his hands more than filled downstairs with Mr. Thorne."

This was the senior surgeon, whose particular line was surgical diseases of the lungs and thorax.

"Good morning, Miss Adams," Guy said. "Mr. Campbell wants me to take off —"

"Mr. Campbell looked in just now," she answered, severely. "While you were with Nurse Shaw."

Her voice implied dalliance. It annoyed Guy.

"The nurses are in a fair tizz this morning," he answered, washing his hands vigorously at the basin on her wall. "Perhaps you haven't heard of the lousy militant porters and their ban on this ward."

"I'm in sympathy with their aims," said the school teacher.

"Then you won't mind sharing the discomforts with the four private patients in the ward, will you? This is an amenity bed, you know, not a pay-bed. Or shall I arrange for you to go down to a general ward?"

She shrank from that. Have a hoard of other women gloating over her injuries, her school problems, the drama of the attack on her? Giving her sympathy, or blame, certainly advice.

"Well, no," she said, groping for lost dignity.

"Don't talk," said Guy, smiling kindly as he began to ease off the plaster strips from her forehead and chin, where the young thug with the beard had struck her face with his ruler for criticising his feeble attempt to construct an intelligible map of his immediate home neighbourhood in a geography lesson.

"Healing nicely," Guy said. "We'll let all the scabs have some air now. I should think you'll be fit to go home the day after tomorrow."

Miss Adams made no answer to this, but as soon as

the registrar had wheeled away the trolley she pulled the small mirror out of her handbag and stared in horror at her altered, hideously marked face. Go home, indeed! Looking like this! Not if she knew it! But put in for compensation and before those 'nicely healing' scabs came off. Note-paper. She had none. Perhaps...

Getting out of bed Miss Adams put on her dressing gown and left her cubicle. She meant to ask young Daphne Parker for paper to write her letter, hospital-headed paper, if possible. Daphne was always writing letters.

But she heard voices in cubicle 2, Dr. Fisher's, of course, cheering up the victim for tomorrow. Perhaps cubicle 3 then.

She parted the curtains gently, to meet the fierce gaze of the frustrated, apprehensive trade union official, Fred Gates.

"Pardon me for intruding," she said, in the slightly gushing voice she used to parents or school offiicials, "but have you by any chance got a sheet of note-paper you could let me have?"

Mr. Gates was astonished.

"Note-paper?" he growled. "Why the hell should I? Who are you, anyway?"

Miss Adams dropped the curtain and moved on. No manners. Ill, perhaps. The voice was peculiar. Now he was coughing.

Dr. Fisher was still with Miss Parker in cubicle 2. Miss Adams peeped into cubicle 1. The other new patient, of course. She made her request, but before Sister Hallet could answer Nurse Shaw arrived, pushing the dressings trolley, now equipped with another set of varied apparatus.

"Excuse me, Miss Adams," Patty said. "I must ask you to go."

"I didn't invite her to come," Miss Hallet protested, pulling herself up in bed and staring at Miss Adams. "Been in the wars, haven't you? What was it? Car crash, I suppose?"

Miss Adams burst into tears, retreated in great disorder and went on to Sister's room. There was no one there but there was a paper rack on the desk with forms for tests, writing-paper and envelopes. Miss Adams helped herself, blew her nose and moved back up the corridor. The newcomer in cubicle 1 was still talking in the same harsh voice. Miss Adams stopped to listen.

"...in those days. Women trained as doctors but they never got consultant jobs except in the few hospitals staffed entirely by women. Or only if they were exceptionally brilliant. The young housemen went for the nurses."

"They still do," Miss Adams heard Patty say, with a slight chuckle.

"Then you'd better be careful. Take care, girl, you're hurting me."

"Sorry. You're so very thin —"

"That'll do. I know what I am. No need to be clumsy. Slipshod. Standards dropping all the time. Every way. When I was a ward sister we had a proper scandal. Nurse killed herself."

"Whatever for?"

"Because we had to dismiss her on account of an affair she had with a Dr. Thompson."

"*Thompson*?" Patty was startled. "Not *our* Dr. Thompson?"

Miss Hallet was annoyed. Her reminiscences were always a long catalogue of other people's failures, chiefly nurses, sometimes doctors: G.P.s who had made fatally wrong diagnoses, consultants who had advised wrong treatments; deaths on the operating table, patients sent home too early, doctors called in too late. With herself a stern angel of the Lord, handing out admonition, sanction, retribution, doom. And this half-trained, happy-go-lucky chit, pulling her up over a totally unimportant slip of the tongue.

"Thompson," she repeated. "The nurse was called Wheeler. It was twenty years ago. I warned the girl. She could have resigned. She had to be dismissed. She chose suicide. Useless, hysterical. Never would have been a proper nurse."

Patty had let the old woman run on in spite of her mounting disgust. She finished the routine in silence and left with her trolley to make the same preparations for operation in the next bed.

Dr. Joan Fisher, who had heard the whole of Miss Hallet's story, got up from the chair at Miss Parker's bedside. She patted the girl's hand.

"Nurse Shaw wants you now, Daphne. Don't let anything worry you. I'll come up tomorrow evening. Mr. Campbell's sure he's on to the right thing."

Outside the ward she met David Thompson coming out of the private room opposite Mrs. Camplin's.

"Does Miss Field want to leave us?" Dr. Fisher asked.

"*She* doesn't. But her boss has her insured for the private bed and he's hopping mad. If they don't put back the telephones up here, he'll insist we move her."

"The whole thing's crazy," Joan said.

He looked at her sharply. She spoke coldly, distantly. Not like the Joan he had begun to rely upon for understanding and comfort. The trouble with the lay staff was a bloody bore, but they were getting organised, volunteers and agency nurses, so what?

Joan said, in a low, serious voice, "There's a new case

in Bed 1. An old ex-sister of this hospital. Ian's doing her tomorrow — exploratory, I think. She talks, far too loud and very scurrilous. She was naming names. It bothered me."

"Why?"

He was still puzzled, by her attitude, her careful, withdrawn manner.

"Joan, what is it? What did she say? Who is she?"

"She told a story, David, about a Dr. Thompson. She is an ex-nurse. Sister Hallet."

She looked up at him. His face had gone white and though he did not move she noticed that the hand he had left on the knob of the private room door had moved from it and tightened into a fist.

Joan went on steadily, "I remembered what you told me when we were discussing poor little Daphne Parker's neurosis. The nurse you had known — the suicide..."

His eyes were blazing into hers. She turned away, sickened. Why had she blurted it all out? Why not keep it to herself? Fool, clumsy fool! He need not have known and she need not have known he was the Thompson old Hallet had slandered just now. Her fault, fool, fool!

She heard him whisper, "Oh, my God!" then he was gone, striding past Hallet's cubicle, to find Fred Gates, union official, poor sod, in for those tests that would probably spell out his lung cancer. It *would* be Hallet, damn her and damn her again!

Mr. Gates stubbed out his tenth cigarette of the day as Dr. Thompson came into his cubicle.

"Smoking isn't allowed up here," David said. "Didn't they tell you?"

"No, doctor," Gates said and added defiantly, "Not that it 'ud 'ave made any difference. I know what you doctors say about tobacco. I spend my life in stuffy rooms, all the blokes puffing away like chimneys. You get to rely on it."

"You'll have to control it if you want to get better," Dr. Thompson told him. "And I mean that. If you can't give it up I'll have to give you up."

He said it with a smile that wiped out Fred's anger, but did nothing to reassure him.

"I'll just examine your chest again," the physician said, helping the man to take off his pyjama jacket. "No, don't lie back. Sit forward."

3

Dr. Thompson arrived at the entrance to the kitchen wing of St. Edmunds Hospital in a flaming temper. He had been forced to walk both up and down the stairs from the third floor to Hunter Ward. Every single one of his medical patients there was suffering from the jitters except the old-fashioned left-wing trades union official, who with his master craftsman's pride and obstinacy distorted by his present position, calmly spoke of the solidarity of working men and women. At the same time he refused to stop smoking because it was an infringement of his rights as a man. Also he just didn't believe what the doctors said about it causing cancer.

"Stupid crack-pot old bugger," Thompson muttered, pausing beside the outer door of the kitchens. "Why come here at all then?"

He pushed his way forward and stood just inside the door of the main kitchen, looking about him, searching for the catering chief officer, whom he had traced here from his office, where the two secretaries were both sulky and unhelpful.

When he had located the man he raised a hand

and beckoned. The catering chief officer hurried across.

"Meals for my patients in Hunter," said Dr. Thompson briefly. "What are you doing about it, Phillips?"

Mr. Phillips raised both hands in a despairing gesture.

"Wells has been along here. I tried to keep him out. He shouted for help and four of my people began to threaten. So I had to let him speak. Seeing most of them don't understand English it can't have had much effect." He giggled nervously.

"You mean they'll do what you tell them?"

He knew, from the caterer's report to the appropriate House Committee, that the kitchen staff held a fine mixture of Spanish, Italian, Irish, Hindu and Moslem, with two or three Englishmen, who never stayed more than a couple of months and were not easy to replace.

"My patients must be fed," he said firmly. "You aren't on the side of these bastards, I hope."

"Certainly not," Phillips said and added in a bitter tone, "After all, my salary is based on the number of meals I provide."

"I know. Disgraceful system, like most things in this bloody so-called service, except the actual treatment."

A small crowd had gradually assembled round the two men at the door. A formidable crowd, Thompson thought, looking at a couple of white-aproned butchers, with their long, sharp knives held in strong, brown hands. He stared at them until their angry eyes shifted, then spoke.

"About Hunter Ward," he said. "I don't give a damn for your political nonsense. My job is to diagnose and try to cure disease. I have to have my patients, all of my patients, in here to get the results of tests. Whether they pay for their beds or not they are entitled to use the Health Service for that purpose because they are citizens paying rates and taxes, most of them National Insurance, too. The hotel side of their stay is not my concern." He paused, then shouted, "Until you lot threaten it and upset them! Do you understand English?"

A few heads nodded, several men, including the butchers, moved away. One thick Irish voice called out, "We're concerned to help the poor against the rich every time, God save them, poor devils, kept waiting on the lists, so they are."

"Bloody nonsense and you know it!" roared Thompson, taking a step towards the man, who shook back his straggling locks and bared his teeth.

"I've just been up to Hunter Ward. My patients there — and you needn't growl at me — my patients there are not all paying. There are only four that are. They are naturally upset and worried. Two of those others, not paying ones, mind you, but given priority for their medical needs, are a social services official and a boy with leukaemia. Are you going to make them worse by your cruel idiocy? A young woman overcome by having to deal with three cases of murdered babies? A boy of fourteen, too old for the children's ward, dying of his disease! Would you have him sent into a men's terminal cancer ward, old men with disgusting conditions and young men in despair? Or in Hunter Ward, allowed to understand his fate by slow degrees, poor kid, with his mother and his friends seeing him as much as they can? Well, is that what you want?"

There was a short silence. Phillips showed clearly that he was afraid the whole kitchen staff might walk out on him. But the Irishman began to shout again and spluttered and choked himself and two fair-haired Scandinavians, who had recently replaced the Englishmen, burst into loud laughter, smote him on the back and pulled him away. The Mediterraneans, who spoke very little English but understood passionate feeling, bowed and moved off. The Far East, who had understood nothing, followed them. Phillips and Dr. Thompson were alone.

"The governors ought to sack the lot, beginning with Joe Wells," said Thompson, watching them go.

"Close the hospital, you mean?"

"If necessary. Let the Ministry cope. It's illegal, what they're doing, after all. Right outside their terms of employment."

Mr. Phillips agreed. "I've been trying to fix something from the office," he said. "Simple menus, no choice or none to speak of. Private firm. Their own apparatus. Usually do weddings and that sort of thing."

"Good. We've got an agency nurse to help out. Hope it won't upset Sister Baker. Medical staff's entirely loyal. So is X-ray and the labs. Some of the path. assistants are doubtful, but Mr. Thorne is having a word with them. Mostly young technicians. They'll depend on references to get higher jobs. No good waving their diplomas about if they muck up their work here."

He left the kitchens tired, indignant, deeply depressed. Not, he had to acknowledge, solely by the illegal, mean, stupidly political slant given to the whole miserable business by the head porter, but by his own unhappy encounter with Joan Fisher. Was she really capable of accepting slander, overheard through cubicle curtains? Malicious evil slander from old Hallet. Ex-Sister Hallet, whose uncontrolled spite and reckless tongue had checked a most promising early career? Of all people his Joan, as he had allowed himself to call her, when their friendship and mutual liking had begun to develop into a joyfully deeper relationship. They were not children, not without experience, personal as well as professional. Besides, they had exchanged the stories of various early events in their lives. Was she suddenly willing to accept another, adverse verdict upon him? Had she always doubted his own account of that early tragedy? The coroner had upheld him when Hallet had tried to blacken him, to destroy his career. And she had not forgotten, evidently. Ill luck had sent her to St. Edmunds, though not, thank God, as his own patient.

He found himself hoping the old harridan was nursing an inoperable cancer. Hadn't Ian said there was nothing very definite but she seemed to have been going downhill for some time before she went to her own doctor, who promptly sent her to the surgeon. So he allowed himself to hope for something fatal.

He wanted her dead, he swore to himself, passionately. Dead and in her grave, her wicked stories buried with her. And Joan, his love, her faith restored, if indeed it had been shaken, safe from doubt in his arms.

As the long day dragged on the confusion and anxiety in Hunter Ward gave place to a certain satisfaction on Sister Baker's part. Some of her worst problems were solved, some of her more alarming fears were proved false. The nurses were magnificent; since that morning they had more than replaced the usual ward maids in washing out the baths and bedpans, as well as dealing with their proper work of caring for the patients, logging their reactions on their charts, making their beds, changing their clothes and suppressing their natural despondency.

Sister Baker joined in their activities. It was she who walked down to the lifts on the next floor, found the Jamaican, Armstrong, who had brought up Mr. Gates the day before, and persuaded him to bring the Hunter Ward trolley of medical supplies up to the fourth floor by standing in front of the control buttons and daring him to move her away. Tim Street, the male nurse in Hunter, was waiting for them. As the porter wheeled out the medical supplies, Tim pushed in the dirty linen. The porter, who had suffered snubbing from his immediate boss, said cheerfully, "You work damn well all out now, man? But Mr. Wells, he tell me, no clean sheets, no food. No —"

"Tell your Mr. Bloody Wells he can stuff —" Tim shouted as the lift doors clanged shut.

"Nurse Street," Sister Baker said, "we won't have that sort of language here, please. Now, listen." She beckoned him into her room and shut the door. "Dr. Thompson has just rung me to say Mr. Phillips has got permission from the governors to engage an emergency caterer for the ward. To avoid picketing at the lifts, this firm will bring their apparatus up the fire-escape, but not until all the non-resident staff have gone home. There won't be enough night staff to picket the back of the hospital as well as the front. They've promised to come before you and Patty go off yourselves."

"Super!" said Tim, rubbing his hands together in glee.

"I'd like you to stand by for their arrival and go down the escape to help them and show the way when I give the word. Very quietly, you understand? And very quickly in case of snoopers. We'd call the police if they did picket the fire-escape, but we want to avoid that sort of confrontation."

Tim nodded. Never the police; he would always agree to that.

"I really don't know what this country's coming to,"

Sister said with great indignation at this extraordinary method of looking after sick people.

Before she went off duty that evening she was able to show the two registrars the new arrangements for defeating the siege of Hunter Ward. The agency nurse, Miss Biggs, had stayed on, prepared to go on night duty. So Sister was able to introduce her to these two senior hospital doctors. They were really assistant consultants, held at an inferior level of status, until recently never given their due in salary or regard. Now, with overtime, they could earn more than fully part-time senior consultants.

The introductions made, the two men took Nurse Biggs on a round of their respective patients, though their respective masters had already done so earlier in the day.

Nurse Biggs made no objection to seeing her charges from a slightly different angle. She was a lively-looking, broad-shouldered woman in her early forties, who seemed to be grimly amused by the challenge this temporary post was offering.

"I was in the Middle East for a time," she told them, "and then I did ten years in an Indian mission. But the climate began to get me down and I came home. I didn't think much of the hospitals outside London and they wouldn't take me back at my old teaching hospital where I trained. So I'm freelance and I'll see how it goes."

"I shouldn't think you'll have any trouble," Trevor Leigh told her. "Do you want to show her your list for Campbell tomorrow, Guy? I'll go and talk to Lionel. Bring Nurse..."

"Biggs, sir."

"Sorry. Nurse Biggs across when she's seen your lot. If the boy's asleep I'll go on to the shop steward."

"Is he?"

"Talks like one. Honestly, I don't know. Not that it matters. His chest is the trouble; smokes like three chimneys and that isn't directly due to his job, or I suppose it could be."

"Stop blathering, Trevor. Come on, Nurse Biggs. You've seen Mrs. Camplin, we needn't go in there, thank God. Mr. Graham, he's a ship's purser, is a nice straightforward hernia. Not for me, this time, I'm afraid. Mr. Campbell wouldn't let me, as he's a paying patient. We'll skip Miss Parker and her appendix, but I think we'd better do a courtesy call on Sister Hallet, exploratory laparotomy, but not much doubt what we'll find, I'd say. True Scottish caution, our Ian always shows."

"That's the retired nurse, isn't it? Sister warned me she might be difficult."

"You can say that again. Treats Patty like mud, but tells her horror stories about nurses seduced by senior staff and drowning themselves."

"Patty? Oh, you mean Nurse Shaw?"

"Patty Shaw. Yes. Second year probationer. Very efficient. Dishy as well."

"I see."

Nurse Biggs found the young man likeable as well as good-looking and capable, but she thought he talked too freely for his own safety. Hospital gossip was unlikely to have changed since her own young days. All institutions suffered from gossip and in a hospital where the supply was rich, often shocking, discretion was needed far more than in school or college or even a large office.

They found Sister Hallet subdued, not a little anxious.

"Sister brought me my tea herself," she said. "Very good of her, but it shows the strike is serious."

"There'll be volunteers to help by tomorrow morning," Nurse Biggs told her, comfortingly, forestalling Guy who had no exact news of this.

"I'm glad to hear it," Miss Hallet said with a bitterness that belied her words. "Not that I'll know much of what's happening tomorrow."

"And by the day after," Guy told her, "you'll find we've got the whole thing sewn up with maximum comfort laid on."

"I hope you sew *me* up with maximum comfort, young man," she answered, giving him such a frosty smile, with so much malice gleaming in her sunken eyes that Nurse Biggs was quite startled.

"I think we'd better go on to Miss Parker, after all," Guy said helplessly. "Then I'll hand you over to Trevor to get the latest low-down on the medical cases. Or perhaps you've already got it all from Sister."

Outside the curtains Nurse Biggs said in a very low voice, "I see what you all mean. Yes, I see quite clearly."

"I thought you might," Guy told her. "Ah, here's Trevor. Just a minute—" He had caught a signal from Patty at the end of the corridor and was gone.

"Bed 3," Nurse Biggs said to Trevor. "A neurotic with a grumbling appendix, Sister told me. They hope to benefit the one by removing the other. Am I right?"

"You are, and I know Miss Parker, too," Trevor said without further comment. "Let's go in."

At the end of the ward Guy said, "You shouldn't interrupt me doing a round. What's up?"

"The fire escape door," Patty said. "I can't shut it."

"Show me."

She did and he explained how it worked as he fastened it up again.

"Now open it," he said.

"Open it? But I just —"

"Show me you know how to open it. Go on. Show me."

"I didn't ask you to help me shut the darned thing just to have a lesson —"

"You need a lesson! Open the bloody door!"

She saw he meant it. She understood why. If there was a fire she must be able to cope. It was months since she had done a fire drill and even then someone else had led the way, she had only had to help a dummy patient go down the escape.

When she had opened and shut the door several times and Guy had watched her wash some oil from her fingers he said, "Someone been loosening off the rust. Why was the door open anyway?"

"To bring up the new caterer's gear. He brought a lovely little portable electric oven with a hot plate on top and a heated trolley like the 'meals on wheels'. Fantastic."

"As long as they don't cut off the power," Guy said as they went back down the ward.

At eight that evening Sister Baker went off duty. The two nurses, Patty and Tim went off duty. The night nurse, Moll Wilson, took over with Nurse Biggs, now reasonably familiar with the ward and its occupants.

It was Nurse Biggs who showed Moll the new kitchen arrangements and offered to get her breakfast ready for her.

"Just tea and toast," Nurse Wilson said. She was far too thin, the agency nurse thought, and too pale, though that went with her dark eyes and hair. And she looked very tired, not a bit as if she had just got up after a good eight hours' sleep. But then last night must have been an anxious time for her, on her own and not knowing if the general services would all be cut off at any minute.

Moll was looking in all the cupboards in the kitchen. No changes there, dressings as usual, linen as usual. The frig? She straightened up, angry, but still listless.

"We're short on milk," she complained. "No use asking them to bring me up some, is there?"

Nurse Biggs shook her head. She had checked the milk herself earlier. She did not think they were likely to be short, but if they collected some now and there was any difficulty in the morning it would do no harm to stock up.

"I'll go down and find some," she said, "if you'll tell me how."

Moll sighed her relief. When she was alone she unlocked her private small locker. A few minutes later she looked at her watch. Those cases for the theatre tomorrow morning, and she hadn't even set eyes on them since she came on duty. So she visited Miss Parker first. The girl's sedation was working nicely; she was drowsy, not at all apprehensive. Nice Mr. Graham was disappointed he was not allowed a nightcap, but was ready to joke about it. Old Miss Hallet had been a bit confused and frightened the night before, having just come in that afternoon. She should be under sedation, too, like Miss Parker.

But Sister Hallet was very wide awake, looking up at Nurse Wilson with bright, inquiring eyes. She said at once, "Don't leave me in the dark, nurse. We don't have to settle down yet, it's barely half-past eight."

"You've got your light on," Moll said. She spoke briskly, covering up the confusion she felt and beginning to turn away. There was something alarming in this queer old woman's voice and manner.

"Don't go, nurse. I'm speaking to you."

Not only speaking but groping under her pillow.

"Now! Bend down a little. There!"

Sister Hallet's pocket torch shone out suddenly, directed straight at Nurse Wilson's face. Then it was clicked off, as suddenly as it had come on.

"I thought as much. Pin-point pupils. Addict, I suppose? Registered? Not likely. Disgraceful! Pin-point pupils and just come on duty."

Moll Wilson gave a loud hysterical laugh, then clapped a hand to her mouth and stared at her accuser. She forced herself to speak calmly.

"Anyone would have contracted pupils with a light shone straight in her eyes."

Her voice was very low, but Sister Hallet heard her and snorted.

"I'd have seen that happen. But no. I know better. Something will have to be done about you, my girl. Danger to the patients. Danger —"

She had spoken in a low voice herself, but so fast that her saliva began to spill from the corner of her mouth, so that she had to fumble for her handkerchief to wipe it away. When she looked up again, Nurse Wilson had gone.

4

THE VOLUNTEER HELPERS arrived at St. Edmunds at nine o'clock exactly on the following morning. There were seven of them altogether, three of whom had been privately approached by the senior lay staff. Two of them were V.A.D.s, local women, accustomed to standing in at holiday times for any useful work in running the wards. The third had been a keen member of the W.V.S. during the war and though she was now nearly seventy had not lost her valuable common sense and level good temper.

These three familiar faces passed the porters' lodge at a sensible matter of fact pace and disappeared into the hospital secretary's office.

Of the remaining four one was a Jamaican woman who went quietly and quickly to the service lift, where she found her porter husband and was taken quickly to the third floor, from where she climbed to Hunter Ward.

The three left behind were not so fortunate. The seven who had gone past the lodge had all arrived at the unusual hour of nine, which was not a visiting hour. They were not recognised as relations of any patient dangerously ill, but seemingly they knew where they were going and why, without needing help or advice. All except these three who stood about, not speaking, but warily alert; who did at last bring Joe Wells to the window of his office. He leaned out to speak to them.

"Can I help you?" he asked and his voice was brusque, full of suspicion.

One of the three stepped towards him. He had a mild face, with a weak beard and receding hair.

"I want to go up to Hunter Ward," he said. "Can you direct me, please?"

"What for?" The head porter drew back to appear again outside the door.

"To offer —" the man began, but he was pushed gently aside by one of the others.

"Press card," the supplanter said briskly. "You the boss of this lark? Turn out the private patients? Cut off the services to them? No pay-beds and all that bollocks?"

"My name is Wells, Joe Wells," the head porter said, his face growing red as his anger rose. "I'm not giving interviews to the likes of you. It's no joke, I can tell you." His rage stopped his breath.

The journalist turned his head towards the one he had supplanted. "Why don't you go on up?" he suggested. "Top floor. Beat it, before —"

Wells roared for help. He shouted his indignation. His pickets had let him down! There'd be hell to pay! What did the lazy buggers think he meant when he told them to stop cars and taxis at the gates of the hospital?

"Pickets?" the journalist asked. "Those chaps out in the road? They didn't stop any of us seven."

"Not stop the cars? The taxis?"

"We walked, old son. Every one of us. Don't all ride in

cars like you wealthy chaps. You'll have to brush up your organisation, won't you?" He suddenly pulled a small camera from his mackintosh pocket and snapped Wells with his mouth open. "Be seeing you," he said and marched out through the incoming rush of the ten failed pickets. He laughed aloud as he went past the hospital gates. Two small boys were busily drawing a very obscene picture on the banner the pickets had left propped against the wall.

Truants from school, he decided and laughed again as the boys ran off.

Meanwhile the last of the new arrivals had quietly followed the bearded one up the stairs. In Hunter Ward, where the patients' day had begun a couple of hours before the volunteers arrived, all was peace. The consultants, both senior and junior, had held a conference with the resident housemen the night before to arrange that all purely medical and surgical treatment for every patient in Hunter, private and amenity, would be carried out as planned.

"And that means we have to have the theatre fully manned, with no snags over the lifts and stretchers," Mr. Campbell insisted. "Theatre 2 has been allocated to me as being the nearest. Theatre Sister and her nurses won't let us down. We'll wheel our own stretchers. I've got three cases on my list from Hunter, two amenity and one private. I propose to take them all down together and Armstrong will bring them up separately. O.K.?"

They all agreed. Armstrong was ready to help in the treatment of sick people whoever they were. Nobody had bothered to explain the situation to him. He knew he had to consider Wells as his boss and he was ready to obey him most of the time for the sake of peace. Besides —

"I shall do Hallet first," Campbell told Guy and the

houseman. "She deserves priority, poor old bag, in spite of her bloody-mindedness. The appendix next, what's her name, Parker. You can scrub-up for that Guy. I must deal with Graham myself, since he came to me privately. I've explained to him about going down with the others. Only fair."

"Did he mind?" Guy asked.

"Laughed. Said the nurses had told him he would be asleep anyhow. Only too pleased to get it over this way. Better than risking the ship's doctor having to cope if his hernia strangulated in the middle of the Atlantic."

To Sister Baker's relief these arrangements went off without any trouble. She was able to do her personal round of the medical patients in the ward.

In Mrs. Mitchell's room she found Mrs. Armstrong sweeping and dusting.

"Aren't I lucky, Sister?" Mrs. Mitchell said. "Mrs. Armstrong came to us at once when she heard of our siege."

The Jamaican's face split into a wide smile. Her magnificent teeth gleamed white in her large black face.

"Mistress Mitchell knew me jus' five minutes after I come in her room," she said proudly.

"I think you had better go now to the cubicles," Sister ordered firmly. "There are two operation cases down in the theatre from Beds 1 and 2 and I want their cubicles swept and dusted in good time before they come up from the theatre."

"Yes, mam," Mrs. Armstrong said, collecting her cleaning aids in one hand and giving a little wave to Mrs. Mitchell with the other.

"What did she mean, you knew her?" asked Sister when the door was shut.

"Just that. The black porter, Armstrong, has brought

me up various parcels of things and flowers from time to time, hasn't he?"

"Yes, but how —?"

"We've had little chats together and he showed me a photograph of himself and his wife taken at home in Kingston before they came to England. I recognised her, of course."

"I'm afraid the black ones all look alike to me," Sister said. She gave a twitch here and there to Mrs. Mitchell's bed cover, plumped up the pillow behind her head, smiled professionally, without meaning, and went away.

Mrs. Mitchell sighed. She had a feeling that the nice, soft-hearted, cheerful Mrs. Armstrong might not be allowed to do her room again. Well, the porter had been very quick off the mark, hadn't he? Voluntary or not, the helpers could not fail to gather fairly substantial rewards, one way or another, for their efforts. Good nature needed support, didn't it? No blame to Mrs. A. Certainly not.

Without in the least altering her approval and liking for Mrs. Armstrong, Mrs. Mitchell pushed her handbag under her mound of pillows. Naturally she had deposited her jewellery in the hospital secretary's office safe. Her gesture was automatic. She had travelled a lot in her time. She knew the world and its inmates. She accepted their varied devious ways and liked most of them.

Not that Sister Hallet, though. Mrs. Mitchell had reached an age at which she did not expect to be snubbed and Sister Hallet had done just that, quite deliberately; it seemed to be a habit with the woman. However, her state of ill-health might account for some of her disagreeableness. Anyway, the poor creature was at this moment undergoing her operation, a serious one,

Mrs. Mitchell reminded herself. She was to be pitied on that account.

In the little waiting room for patients' friends and relations Daphne Parker's mother sat trying to look at an out-of-date magazine while she waited for her daughter to come back from the operating theatre. The surgeon himself had come up to Hunter Ward very early that morning, to make sure Daphne had been properly prepared. The girl had been very drowsy, perfectly calm. Sister had told her all this when she herself reached the ward an hour ago. They expected Daphne back from the theatre any time now.

The door of the waiting room opened softly. A figure in a white hospital overall came in, carrying a cup of coffee.

"Sister Baker thought you might like to have this," she said, putting the cup down on the central table in the little room.

"Are you one of the nurses?" Mrs. Parker asked. The woman was short and thick-set, with short straight grey hair. Not an attractive face, Mrs. Parker thought; in fact, decidedly plain. But her eyes were bright, she looked alert, her voice was gentle, full of sympathy.

"No, I'm just a V.A.D. come to help out in this emergency," she said.

She looked round her and went on, "Only you? The ward has three cases for operation this morning."

Mrs. Parker smiled. She had been up often enough visiting Daphne to hear the ward gossip about the other two.

"One of them's a private patient, an officer of some sort in the merchant navy. I haven't met him, he hasn't left his room since he came in, I believe. But I think his family lives near Liverpool. Too far to come up to town.

It isn't an urgent case, the male nurse says. He came south to have his operation because the waiting lists are very short in the London area. Plenty of doctors. Plenty of beds. Besides, it might turn dangerous, Nurse Street says, at any time."

"I thought you said he was a private patient."

"Insured with B.U.P.A. He has to know in advance when he can be fit again to join his ship."

She drank her coffee quickly, because it was not very hot and handed the cup back to the V.A.D.

"Thank you, nurse. May I know your name?"

"Norris, dear. Mary Norris. There now! I think I can hear the stretchers coming into the ward."

In fact she had heard nothing, but she was determined not to miss the return of the two amenity bed cases. Poor Mrs. Parker with that hysterical girl, but such a devoted mother, who must have spoiled her as a child. And poor Mr. Graham, whose wife had not bothered to fly down from Liverpool. Private patient, so why couldn't she afford it. Or didn't want to come, more likely. That old Hallet, too. But *she* never did have any relations, and for friends, with her reputation in the hospital and the town —

Miss Norris was tidying up the two empty cubicles when the patients came back from the theatre, so she was able to help Sister Baker and the house surgeon and the other V.A.D. to transfer them back to their beds and begin their routine post-operative treatment.

Nurse Shaw was attending Dr. Thompson in his medical round during this time and Nurse Street was with the cosmetic surgeon, helping to change the dressings on Mrs. Zia Camplin's face while listening to her complaints and fears and half-hearted threats to leave the hospital.

"Can't I see what I look like now?" she kept repeating. "Why don't you let me see? Is it too awful? Have you made a — what you call it — a boob?"

"No, I have not," her distinguished London surgeon told her, calmly, dispassionately, "and I am not going to let you see your face until the end of the week. Stop talking now or you'll infect the new dressings I'm putting on."

She was silent at that and the work was finished quickly. To her surprise she had suffered no pain throughout the proceedings and her face did now feel rather more as if it belonged to her in part and might perhaps become wholly hers in time.

The large dark eyes took on an alarmingly arch expression.

"You make me feel you just carve a puppet or make a clay model, not human at all."

This was in truth a very just estimate of the surgeon's regard for Mrs. Camplin. But he only gave her a thin smile and said to Guy Harper, who was standing behind Nurse Street, "See she behaves herself till Saturday," and to the patient, "You're doing very nicely."

Then he was gone and the registrar followed. Nurse Street wheeled the trolley away. Mrs. Camplin stretched out a languid hand to her television set.

The agency nurse came on duty that night with special instructions from Sister Baker, before she left, to give particular attention to the leukaemia boy, Lionel, to Beryl Field, the social services official, and to Mrs. Hurst, the local mayor's mother-in-law, who had been given an amenity bed more in honour of his office than for anything seriously the matter with her. Bed 8 was still empty, even for this kind of concession. The word had gone round the general wards of a threat of starvation upstairs. Also the secretaries were not bothering to send letters to new patients, marked for amenity.

The three operation cases were comfortable, Sister explained. Nurse Wilson would cope with them. Miss Hallet, conscious now but very weak, was on a drip. If Nurse Wilson wanted help for any one of them, it might be for Hallet. The other two had come round normally from their anaesthetics and gone off to sleep with pain-killing sedatives.

Nurse Biggs followed her instructions. She was experienced and very competent; she had no trouble in calming the fears of the social worker who thought that industrial trouble among the hospital lay staff might cut short this blessed interlude away from the parents of battered babies, thieving four-year-olds, truants from school and other unsocial individuals. Her opposite neighbour in Bed 4, the savaged school teacher, whose cuts were now nearly healed, had talked at length to her about their mutual problems. It had not proved anything, but she had not suffered a single nightmare during the last week. Nurse Biggs added comfort and reassurance to both misused, devoted workers.

It was at about eleven o'clock when the agency nurse was summoned by Fred Gates in Bed 3. He had tried very hard to settle down, but his cough and the strange surroundings had again defeated him.

Nurse Biggs dealt with his pillows and his bedclothes, helped him into a new position in the bed, emptied his urine bottle and gave him another and went off to get something in the way of a palliative for the cough and the sleeplessness.

Nurse Wilson was not at the night nurse's desk in the ward corridor nor in Sister's room outside the ward.

Nurse Biggs, who had found Moll Wilson unpleasantly silent, even sulky, when they met as they came on duty, did not bother to search for her, but collected from the ordinary drug cupboard for simple remedies a dose of cough linctus and a few aspirin-type tablets. Back with Mr. Gates, watching him sip the cough mixture and swallow the pills she heard movement in the first two cubicles, one after the other, and the following conversation.

From Bed 1, in Sister Hallet's grating voice, "It's you, is it? Up to your tricks again, I suppose?"

The answer was a whisper, "No. Just your injection."

Nurse Wilson giving the horrid old woman her shot of pain-killer, the agency nurse decided. She heard the curtains of Bed 2 rustle. Miss Parker was evidently too drowsy for conversation.

When Mr. Gates stopped coughing and let his head rest sideways against the pillows that held him sitting forward, Nurse Biggs took the linctus glass to wash it. She found Nurse Wilson in the ward kitchen getting their midnight dinner out of the fridge to warm it up. They both approved of the emergency outside cooking, though Nurse Biggs was used to very good food in the nursing homes and clinics where she usually worked.

After the meal they settled down. The ward seemed quiet enough. Nurse Biggs dozed in a chair in Sister's room, with the door open.

At a little after two she was roused by a confusion of sound. Loud above the ringing of bells, the cries and the shouts, came the high screams of Daphne Parker in an extreme of hysteria.

Nurse Biggs shot out of Sister's room. Moll Wilson was slumped over the night nurse's desk, her head on her arm. Nurse Biggs clutched the head by the cap and the hair and lifted it.

"*Drugs!* oh, my *God*!" she told herself, running down the ward to silence Daphne Parker. The old-fashioned remedy was the best, she decided, and slapped the girl's face hard.

The effect was immediate. Daphne, mouth open, stared unseeing.

"Lie down! You'll pull your clips out!" Nurse Biggs ordered. "Now what possessed you —?"

But Daphne was sobbing quietly and did not settle until after Nurse Biggs had given her another pain-killing dose. Much later in the day she was able to explain to the houseman that it was the pain, the frightful, unbearable pain in her side that had broken her nerve. No one believed her, of course.

The rest of the patients relaxed when the screaming stopped and they understood there was no invasion by militant hospital lay staff come to throw them out into the night.

All except Sister Hallet. Nurse Biggs went straight to her cubicle when she had calmed Miss Parker. She left Moll Wilson staggering uncertainly round the other cubicles.

Sister Hallet lay flat and still, gaunt and straight and grey-faced as she had lain when she arrived back in the ward from the theatre. The drip was still operating, but the fluid was welling out over the canula.

For the circulation had stopped. Sister Hallet was dead.

5

A POST-MORTEM WAS carried out at the hospital at ten o'clock that morning. Dr. Tyne, pathologist, North Country, determined, performed the whole job himself, his large-featured face growing noticeably grimmer as he discovered the extent of the neglect suffered by this part of the department in the last two weeks.

Mr. Campbell was there to watch, also Guy Harper and the surgical houseman, Bob Frost, who offered to do the usual technician's part, but was refused.

"Quicker to get on with it myself," Dr. Tyne told him, "than waste my breath telling you to hand me this and that when I don't know where the hell Smith has put them."

He went on working, rapidly, skilfully and then said, continuing his thought, "After all these years in the P.M. room I'd never have believed Smith would let me down. My lab boys are loyal so far."

"Know which way their bread's buttered," suggested Mr. Campbell. "The whole thing makes me sick."

The angry silence continued until Dr. Tyne had finished and reported morosely, "Nothing here except what you know already, Campbell. Inoperable, really. Best thing for her to go like this."

"But unexpected," the surgeon protested. "I've got to know *why* she went like that. I saw her with Sister Baker just after seven. Blood pressure near normal. Pulse steady. She was doing fine." He paused, then said, with obvious reluctance. "There was no indication then, or in the findings the nurses recorded up to midnight to suggest the circulation failed. So what did?"

Dr. Tyne said roughly, "You'd like it to be something wrong with the drip? Is that it?"

"Or the injections? Mr. Brentford isn't having an easy time in the pharmacy."

"But all that's foolproof, isn't it? You're not suggesting — ?"

"I'm not suggesting anything. But I think we might check. I propose to make a very close inquiry into the after-care, hour by hour."

"While I examine the drip, I suppose? Who set it up?"

Bob Frost said in a low voice, "I did, sir."

Dr. Tyne made a grimace, but it was not ill-natured. "And I must look at her blood for anything odd in *it*?"

"I'm sorry, Tyne. I know you're overloaded. We all are. But don't you see, if this *was* a piece of carelessness due to these brainless louts' behaviour, I'll have something definite to rock the authorities with and make the headlines."

"He'll do just that," whispered Guy to Bob as they followed their master from the room. "Are you sure you didn't slip old Hallet an extra whack of something when you manhandled her back into her bed?"

The houseman, already half asleep, for he had been up most of the night before with two emergency admissions, shook his head violently, more to clear the drowsiness from his mind than in protest at Guy's suggestion. But he was startled, too.

"O.K., Bob," the latter reassured him, remembering those emergency admissions. "But Campbell's on the warpath. You'd better be up in Hunter pretty soon. I'm taking him up there now."

Bob walked rapidly away, while Guy joined the surgeon at the lifts, commandeered one that was empty and before Wells, who was on the phone in his lodge, could interfere, had pressed the button for Hunter Ward, which closed the door.

As they arrived there, Guy said, "Shall I leave the lift open, Mr. Campbell?" The surgeon grinned, but shook his head.

"My colleagues would take a very dim view of that. No, it's a free for all. And I've only got three cases up here altogether. No, two without Hallet."

"Three, sir, with Miss Adams."

"Who's she? No, don't tell me. Savaged schoolmarm."

"Yes, Mr. Campbell. Face injuries from an attack by a teenage kid in class. Superficial. I'd like to discharge her, if you agree. Bed 4."

They had been walking into Hunter Ward after they left the lift and now Sister Baker, hearing voices, hurried out to meet them.

"Good morning, Sister," Mr. Campbell said and went on, without stopping, "Mr. Harper wants me to discharge Miss Adams. Do you agree she's fit and willing to go? I saw her myself last week. I'll have another look now."

"Willing? I should just think so," Sister said. "Up to yesterday she was afraid to take her scars out of her cubicle. This morning she's planning to get her married sister to bring in an anorak with a hood and her dark glasses and a wide scarf to put over the rest of her face. The sister wants her to stay at their home and can take her away in their car."

All these arrangements were repeated with various unnecessary explanations by Miss Adams, while Mr. Campbell gazed at her scars, nicely and cleanly dry, but showing only too plainly the brutal extent of the attack on her.

When she showed signs of beginning to repeat her plans from the beginning, he bent down to touch her face which stopped her talking.

"You'll do," he said. "Don't try to pick off the scabs. Most of them won't leave any mark at all. Don't try fancy ointments and so on. What about going back to school? And compensation? Going to prosecute the young thug's parents?"

"Oh no. I wouldn't dare! Nor would the headmaster. No one ever does do anything."

She saw the disgust on their faces and went on.

"But I've resigned from that school. If I don't get another in a country area I shall emigrate."

"Good luck to you," said Mr. Campbell, asking as he turned to go, "Were you disturbed at all last night when the patient in Bed 1 was taken worse?"

"When Sister Hallet died, you mean? The noise that girl made did wake me, not poor Sister Hallet. But I've no complaint at all about the nursing, doctor. Or the treatment. You've all been splendid. It's those threats downstairs. I'd rather leave — not be a nuisance."

Mr. Campbell thanked her, shook her hand, told Guy to make all the arrangements and went back down the ward to Sister's room, where she was waiting for him and had been joined by Bob Frost.

"Miss Adams has nothing to tell us, Sister." Mr.

Campbell said, accepting the cup of coffee she had prepared for him personally. "Too far away in Bed 4 and asleep, she says, until the Parker girl screamed. But what about *her*? I haven't seen her yet. I wanted to get your report first."

"Yes."

Sister Baker repeated, with full detail, her account of the return to the ward of Sister Hallet and the patient's satisfactory response to the early intensive care given her.

"Yes, yes." Campbell was growing impatient. "It's that appendix case I'm asking you about. Gave trouble in the night, I believe."

"As to that I think you had better see Nurse Biggs," Sister told him. "She said she'd wait up till you came. I'll ring for her, shall I?"

"Please do. And I'll have a word with the hernia chap while we're waiting. No trouble there, I take it?"

"No," answered Sister, with such a severe look on her face that Mr. Campbell wondered what had happened to the least complicated case of the three he had operated upon the day before.

He soon discovered the trouble. Mr. Graham, peacefully isolated in his private plywood cubicle, free from discomfort of any kind, feeling rested after a good night, followed by a limited but reasonable breakfast, looked up from his morning newspaper, as the surgeon shut the door behind him.

"How are you?" Campbell asked.

"I'm fine. Couldn't be better."

"No complaints? I see you've got a newspaper. Congratulations."

Mr. Graham frowned, looked embarrassed, but said, "With the treatment, none whatever. Armstrong's wife brought me in the paper." He hesitated, then went on, "I'd like to make it clear I'm a normally very good sleeper. That's why I told Sister she could cancel any more pills or injections she had lined up for me. She may have told you without explaining."

"Sister Baker said nothing of the kind. Just that you were comfortable."

Mr. Graham laughed, felt a twinge of pain in his lower abdomen and checked his mirth, looking contrite.

Campbell nodded, smiling.

"You see," he said. "Result of boasting. But you want to tell me something, don't you? Something you mentioned to Sister."

"Right. The night nurse. The young one, not Nurse Biggs, she's excellent. Young one, dark, untidy hair, uncertain speech — I travel, you know, east and west — crews all sorts of nationalities. I recognise a junky when I see one."

Mr. Campbell showed neither surprise nor anger.

"I see," he said. "Are you making a formal complaint that the night nurse in attendance on you last night was under the influence of a narcotic drug?"

"That's right," said Mr. Graham cheerfully. "And I don't want her handing me out anything in that line in case she's been mixing things up, if you get my meaning."

Mr. Campbell thought for a few seconds before he replied. Then he said, "I'll see the thing's investigated, here in the ward and down in the pharmacy. You realise it's an extremely serious matter? I hope you haven't spoken about it to anyone but Sister and me."

"Of course not. But you had to know, hadn't you? After what's been going on up here? That poor old girl slipping her anchor —"

Campbell nodded. In spite of his professionally calm face and manner he was really very much upset. He went back to Sister's room determined to start a full inquiry into Nurse Wilson's record. He found that Sister Baker had been called to Bed 2 by Dr. Joan Fisher. But Nurse Biggs was sitting at Sister's desk and got up as he entered.

"Good of you to wait up for me," he said. "I hear you had a pretty ropey night in the ward, one way and another. Sit down, nurse. Finish your coffee."

"Thank you, sir. It's Sister's coffee. I don't want anything."

As the surgeon flung himself into an uncomfortable wicker armchair near the window of the room, Nurse Biggs sat down again, pushed the coffee cup away and began at once her story of the night's events.

"You were with one of the medical cases when you heard Sister Hallet speak?" Mr. Campbell asked.

"Yes, sir. Mr. Gates in Bed 3."

"But that's two cubicles away from Sister Hallet. Yet you heard a conversation in Bed 1?"

"I did. Sister Hallet had a very carrying voice; I'm sure you will have noticed it."

The surgeon nodded.

"Go on."

"The voice was weak, but quite distinct. She said, 'It's you, is it? Up to your tricks again, I suppose?' And Nurse Wilson said, 'No. Just your injection.' "

"You did not see Nurse Wilson?"

"I saw her when we came on duty. I saw her when I'd finished my round of the medical cases and later when —"

"Yes, yes. I meant did you see her come out of the cubicles, Beds 1 and 2?"

"No, but I heard her speak — very low, but quite

distinct, Mr. Gates heard her, too. The ward was perfectly quiet at that time. I know he heard her because he turned his head to look in that direction."

"Didn't Nurse Wilson say anything to Miss Parker?"

"No. But the girl murmured a little and I expect she didn't want to rouse her while she gave her the injection."

Again Mr. Campbell nodded. He got to his feet.

"Thank you, nurse," he said. "You must get off to bed. I needn't tell you to keep your mouth shut about last night and particularly about Nurse Wilson. As you know we're desperately shorthanded."

Nurse Biggs understood him. "You mean —?"

"I mean Nurse Wilson appeared to be perfectly well this morning when she came off duty and she will be coming on duty tonight as usual."

He saw the astonishment and indignation in the agency nurse's face.

"But," he went on, "Sister Baker will give *you* the keys of both drug cupboards this evening and you will administer all doses as written up and signed for by the consultants or the registrars."

Nurse Biggs looked somewhat but not wholly relieved. It would be embarrassing, with Moll Wilson probably desperate for a fix, unless she had a private source of supply.

Mr. Campbell gave her some parting comfort.

"I'm very grateful for your willing co-operation, nurse," he told her. "I needn't tell you we're having a full check on the pharmacy side; all drugs supplied to the ward, books and records examined, — the lot."

He paused again as he reached the door.

"I propose to play it on a day to day basis," he said finally and vanished.

Sister Baker came in directly afterwards. Nurse Biggs stared at her. Already she regretted taking this post. She felt she was being imposed upon. She had agreed to help out at this N.H.S. hospital because the patients and medical staff were being abused by ignorant, wickedly-led, lay staff, who envied the superior skills of trained doctors and nurses and the thought and foresight of people who chose to insure themselves for hospital treatment. And already what had she found? A night nurse who was clearly an addict, a patient dead from no immediately discovered cause. Elderly, with inoperable cancer. Why the fuss? The added fuss after her own report about Moll Wilson. She shivered, rubbing her cold hands together.

Sister said kindly, "Now off you go, nurse. A hot bath and a hot drink in bed. I'll see it comes to you. Sugar?"

"One lump. But nothing else, please, Sister. Or I might not wake up in time for duty."

They both laughed.

Mr. Campbell remembered, as soon as he had left Sister's room, that he had not yet seen the tiresome girl in Bed 2, whose screams had so much upset most of the patients in Hunter Ward. He went along to the second cubicle and looked in. Daphne Parker was listening to Dr. Joan Fisher, who sat at her bedside, holding her hand.

Dr. Fisher released the hand when she saw the surgeon and began to get up, but he waved her down and approached the bed.

"Feeling better this morning, Miss Parker?" he asked. "No more bad dreams?"

The patient giggled feebly but said nothing.

"She's sorry she made a disturbance," Joan said. "D'you want to examine her?"

"No, no." Campbell glanced at the chart at the foot of the bed, nodded and smiled.

"You'll be up in a chair tomorrow," he said, "and on your feet the day after. And you won't have any more tummy upsets, unless you eat too many sweets between meals."

He went away promising himself to ask Joan if she had anything useful to tell him about this difficult girl. The appendix had shown signs of former attacks with a few adhesions, but patients who were determined to enjoy ill-health usually managed to do so once they had formed the habit of it.

On the next day the pathologist reported that Sister Hallet had died from a heavy overdose of a narcotic drug. The coroner was informed and an inquest was ordered.

6

Patty Shaw looked at herself in the long mirror on the door of her small wardrobe. All the rooms in the Nurses Home had built-in cupboards, with shelves and narrow wardrobes. She had put on her pale green trouser suit; it had white facings at the neck of the jacket and three-quarter length sleeves below which her frilled white silk shirt fell to her wrists. Hiding the red roughness there, she decided, making a face at herself as she turned away.

But her appearance did not worry her. She knew she was pretty; not a raging beauty, just pretty and reasonably attractive, with a good figure well displayed by the trouser suit. Altogether quite up to Guy Harper's approval, for surely that must be the reason for his unexpected invitation.

"Will you have dinner with me this evening or tomorrow?" he had asked her that morning.

She had pretended she did not remember her dates just long enough to allow her heart to stop its instant wild gallop. She bent her head over a pocket diary she always carried, hoping to cool her instantly burning cheeks before looking up at him.

She had said, "Yes. Thank you. Where?" in her usual calm, cheerful voice.

Guy said gravely, "I'll pick you up at the Home. I'll book a table at The Patio if that suits you."

She had nodded, looked at her watch and said, with a good imitation of urgent hurry, "Be seeing you," and darted away into the ward kitchen.

Well, here she was and the miracle she had forbidden herself to hope for was about to take place. Going out with Mr. Harper. Guy Harper.

Even Tim, the male nurse, had diagnosed her excitement, though he had not, thank heaven, guessed the author of it.

"Dark horse, Patty," he told her. "Hiding up the boyfriend as if he didn't exist."

"Whoever said he did, nosey?"

"O.K. O.K. Have a ball. Time we all did. I'd like to see those bastards —"

She was ready ten minutes before the given time, but waited in her room until she was five minutes late, so that she clattered down the two flights of uncarpeted stairs to find Guy standing in the hall.

"Sorry, Mr. Harper," she said, genuinely breathless.

"Not to worry."

He guided her to his car with a hand under her elbow. As they settled themselves and he helped her with her seat belt he said, smiling, "Away from that place, Patty, it's Guy."

She laughed.

"In Hunter Ward, Guy, it's been Patty since the emergency began. But I won't forget in Hunter, *Mr.* Harper."

They both laughed.

The Patio was a small Italian restaurant, unpretentious, with a full choice on the printed menu, but an excellent table d'hôte meal of the day. To Patty it seemed perfect, she need not display her relative ignorance of eating places other than cafés, snack bars and occasional visits with her parents to the larger London houses of Lyons and Fortes.

At first their conversation was exploratory; family connections, geographical, educational, athletic, recreational. All quite interesting, Patty decided, but far from exciting. Guy was attentive, pleasant, even amusing from time to time. But it did occur to her to wonder, as they finished their main course and he urged her to choose one of the elaborate puddings on the trolley the waiter pushed forward, to wonder why on earth Guy was giving her this meal when he obviously didn't care a blind bit who she was, what she was, why she was — oh yes, she was attracted all right, but Guy ...

In desperation when the coffee arrived she stopped the mutual catalogue and began to talk about the latest news in the hospital, particularly in the ward. Sister Hallet's death. An overdose, but how come?

"I'm glad you feel you can talk about it," Guy said, with such evident relief and eagerness that her outraged vanity shouted to her heart. "There you are! That's why you're here! To give him the low-down on something that shouldn't have happened and may muck up his career if he slipped up somewhere along the line."

Aloud she said, "Why not? Are you specially worried?"

"In a way, yes. The inquest may be a bit tricky."

"How?"

He stared at her.

"*How*? Because either there was gross carelessness in giving her the right after treatment or the pethidine ampoules had the wrong dose in them, or someone for some reason unknown, bumped off the old woman on purpose."

"Oh gosh! I never thought of that! Surely not? Who, for Pete's sake?"

"She was a legend, apparently, for vicious scandal-mongering and general bloody-mindedness."

Patty nodded, very serious now and beginning to be afraid.

"She did manage to upset the ward, even in two days. Sister couldn't stand her. Nice old Mrs. Mitchell got the brush-off and was hurt about it. Mrs. Armstrong, you know, the black porter's wife, volunteer orderly, was told by Hallet she wouldn't have a nigger cleaning her cubicle. Luckily Mrs. Armstrong doesn't insult easily. She just laughed and dusted along the top of the bed behind Sister Hallet's head."

"Good for her," Guy applauded, beaming at Patty.

She felt encouraged. The approval was not only for the story, some at least was for her way of telling it.

"Then there was her warning to me. But that involved a real libel. I'd better not repeat it."

"You better had, Patty. I won't pass it on unless it becomes, well, important. I may have heard it already, actually."

"It's about one of the consultants."

"Thompson."

"How did you know?"

"Never mind. What did old Hallet tell you?"

"To be careful how I behaved with senior staff. Medical staff, not non-medical. Roughly, apart from the general warnings, I was to be specially cagey over Dr. Thompson because in her day, when he was a junior registrar, he'd had an affair with a probationer and let her down and she'd killed herself."

Guy made no answer for some time. The waiter came up to offer more coffee which both of them accepted. Guy asked for his bill. Patty began to regret her disclosure. He clearly didn't like it, probably didn't like her for blurting it out so baldly. Again she blamed him bitterly for his arrogance and for the dismal failure of this whole encounter. Except the lovely, lovely food, she told herself and laughed aloud at her schoolgirlish simplicity.

That roused him.

"What's so funny?" he asked, sharply, looking up in the middle of pulling notes out of his wallet.

"Basically you," she answered, in sudden anger. "No. I'm sorry. That was rude. I'm sorry."

"Explain."

"No. Scrub it."

He saw tears gather in her grey-green eyes. He remembered she had been grossly over-worked for the last week and blamed himself for treating her with less than usual consideration. Old Hallet's fault again, damn her! Even dead, here they were, making rings round her case. The story about David Thompson, in one of its many forms, was not news, but to have it in this malignant shape, raked up again! Could Thompson really have been so shocked or enraged or both that he had decided to stop that malicious mouth at once? Patty was speaking again, rather huskily.

"You don't think Dr. Thompson ...?"

He pushed back his chair.

"Of course not. Fantastic. Some muddle with the doses. That V.A.D. The old one."

"Miss Norris? Not possible. She helped get Hallet back into bed, then Sister sent her away, while we set up the drip. Miss Norris didn't touch anything on the trolley. She was the other side of the bed."

They left The Patio with smiles and thanks to the waiter and Patty thanking Guy a bit late. Neither spoke much on the way back to the Nurses Home. Guy got out to open the car door for her, saw her politely to the entrance, not yet locked, saw her go inside, received, as she turned to him, her repeated genuine thanks with a natural smile and as she disappeared behind the closing door ran down the steps to his car and drove away.

His flat felt unnaturally empty; cold too. He had always preferred to live alone, the only way to get any reading done in the evenings. Tonight he did not want to do any reading. He wanted to think about Patty. No, about what she had told him. No news, really, but it did put Thompson in the picture. In a picture of possible crime, probably not at all the right one. It had upset Patty, though. A shame, he hadn't intended to upset her. Green eyes went rather well with dark hair. She had resented his concentration on the Hallet case, but she had enjoyed the meal, as well she should, why not, it was a good meal and had cost him a packet. No joke, these days, taking a girl out. What a blessing the Angel had finally walked out on him. Angelina Bass-Wilkins. Never really his cup of tea. Properly scared over his latest idea of emigrating. Well, well. Green eyes, — made a change from frosty blue.

Definitely, green, thought Patty, with regret, studying her eyes in the mirror in her small bed-sitter in the Nurses Home. What the hell! Guy only wanted her help over that old hag's overdose. And she had been able to tell him nothing, really. How could she? She was off duty from eight. The mistake, or the wickedness, if that was it, was after she'd left the ward. Must have been.

In Hunter Ward the next morning Daphne Parker was slowly responding to Dr. Joan's gentle persuasion.

"Mr. Campbell is very pleased with you," Joan told her, "but he is worried about your...your attack...in the night."

"My nightmare," said Daphne sulkily. "He wouldn't let me explain. Nor even apologise for upsetting the ward."

"Explain to me," suggested Joan. "Tell me about your recovery from the time you woke up after the operation to when this dream frightened you."

Miss Parker was perfectly willing to oblige. She gave a dramatic account of emerging from the anaesthetic and hearing Sister Baker reassuring her and then of sinking gently down into another kind of sleep.

"And then?" prompted Joan.

"I woke up and it was dark and the night nurses had come on. The young one, Nurse Wilson, brought me a hot drink and made me use the bedpan, which hurt a lot, but I needed it. She didn't say much. When I asked her how Sister Hallet was she said, 'Bad,' and added, not meaning me to hear her, I think, 'Serve the old bitch right!' "

"Are you sure?" Joan asked, shocked at such a lapse on the nurse's part.

"Quite sure," Daphne insisted, with a spiteful tone in her voice, "and not surprising seeing the way Sister Hallet scolded her the night before."

"How?" Joan asked, half persuaded now that the girl was speaking the truth for once.

"Called her a drug addict. I heard her distinctly. I'm not really surprised. Nurse Wilson has been peculiar every night since I came up to this ward."

Dr. Fisher got to her feet. This must be stopped. The

girl was getting excited; probably everything she had said was a half-lie, a gross exaggeration. It must go no further.

Daphne watched her. She saw the doctor's uncertainty. She was accustomed to seeing doubt grow in the faces of her listeners.

"You haven't let me tell you about the nightmare," she complained in a whining voice. "I thought that was what you wanted to hear."

Joan was exasperated. She said, half angry, half joking, "I suppose you thought Sister Hallet was coming into your cubicle to attack you!"

Daphne stared at her in horror. She slid down in the bed, pulling the sheet up till it half-covered her face.

"How did you know?" she whispered. "It was just that. An old, old face, white hair, wicked old eyes, leaning down over me. An old hand on my arm, sharp nails pressing into my skin. I screamed and screamed —"

"And Nurse Biggs ran into your cubicle and there was no one there. *There was no one there.* Nurse Wilson was at the night nurse's desk. Sister Hallet wasn't in your cubicle. She was already dead."

"I dreamed it, then," Miss Parker said, repentant now, looking pathetic and helpless.

But Dr. Joan Fisher had gone, hurrying down to the general medical ward for men, where she hoped to find Dr. Thompson.

He had just left it when she got there, but the staff nurse told her he was making for the similar ward for women. Here she had to wait, but she did not mind. There was time to arrange her thoughts about Daphne's outpourings. She was inclined to believe Sister Hallet's reported accusation of Nurse Wilson. The rumours about the night nurse in Hunter Ward were spreading.

This seemed to confirm them sufficiently to push on a proper investigation. David must be told, clearly and shortly; it might be his duty to take action, or at least warn the senior medical consultant, Dr. Thorne.

He listened to her account with the same unbending reserve he had shown in all their short encounters since her stupid outburst on the day Sister Hallet had displayed to Patty her decaying but still venomous fangs.

"I don't quite see how it concerns *me*," he said at last. "Surely it is for the Senior Nursing Officer to look after the nurses, make her own inquiries about their behaviour and take the right action."

"But this may have great importance at the inquest," Joan urged.

"And it can have nothing to do with *me*," he insisted. But seeing her face change from persuasion to pleading he relented enough to ask in a gentler voice, "Why should it? Why should you think I come into it? Why should you care if I do?"

"Because I do," she answered desperately. "I do care, David."

He put a hand on her arm.

"I'm due in Out-patients in five minutes," he said, almost breathlessly, his eyes searching hers. "I'll pick you up at your place at seven. Tell me then where you'd like to have dinner."

At home, she decided, happily; they'd dine at home. She tried to remember what she had in the deep freeze at her flat and what she must get on her way down there when she had finished her day's work at St. Edmunds.

David made no fuss about it when he found she was not waiting for him in the hall of the block of flats, but wearing an apron and a face flushed from cooking in answer to his ring on her bell.

"You said I was to tell you where we'd have dinner," she said as she let him in. "Well, it'll be here. I owe you at least one meal, I'm sure. If only as an apology."

"What's that for?"

"My stupidity the other day when I overheard Sister Hallet haranguing Nurse Shaw. It was a kind of panic. What an evil old woman Hallet really was."

He had moved on into her small sitting room, but when she spoke of the dead ex-nurse he stopped short, standing with his back to her. His voice was cold as he asked, "Must we really talk about her?"

"Yes," Joan said, driven beyond control. "I won't have her coming between you and me. Can't you understand that? You didn't *have* to tell me about that wretched neurotic girl who fell for you and got no encouragement and pretended you had let her down, egged on by Hallet. And was such a nuisance she was sacked for neglecting her work and went away and drowned herself. You didn't *have* to tell me that story, but, my God, I'm beginning to understand the kind of brush-off you can lay on! Oh, heck! There's the soup boiling over! Help yourself to a drink and pour me a sherry."

She was gone, but not out of hearing for she heard the great, relieving and relaxing laugh with which he wheeled about to watch her dash from the room.

When she had regained control over her cooking and came back she found that David had poured the drinks and was standing beside the table. He opened his arms to her and she went to them without hesitation in full confidence.

The cooking suffered not a little; the soup had to be abandoned but neither minded much about that, for David insisted upon taking her out after all. It was not until after he had brought her home again and lingered, talking about possible future plans, that he suddenly spoke again about the coming inquest.

"The main evidence will relate to Nurse Wilson," he said. "The pharmacy have a complete fool-proof report, Dr. Tyne's autopsy is quite definite the woman died of an overdose of narcotic. Accident probably, due to negligence, incapacity, or something of the sort."

"Not deliberate?" Joan said, worried again on behalf of Moll Wilson. "There was provocation. Moll openly hated the old woman."

"So did I," David said smiling. "But it would never have occurred to me to murder her."

It was splendid, Joan thought, that he could say that so easily, so cheerfully.

"Of course not, darling," she told him. "But it's possible someone did and it could be poor Mollie. Addicts are emotionally very unstable, aren't they?"

"Like hell, they are," he agreed. He was ready that evening to agree with anything his love said to him, even this rather dangerous suggestion.

7

NURSE WILSON, CALLED before the Senior Nursing Officer and the Night Sister, with Sister Baker also in attendance, defended herself with unlooked-for skill. She agreed that she was asleep when Miss Parker had her so-called nightmare. She had been completely exhausted by all the extra work in Hunter Ward of the last three days. Yes, in spite of having the experienced Nurse Biggs to help her. Why? Because of course she had had to take Nurse Biggs round the whole ward as well as doing her normal duties.

"Nurse Biggs had met all the patients already," Sister Baker interrupted. "She arrived early and agreed at once to take night duty straight away."

"I was overtired," Nurse Wilson insisted. "I had a ghastly headache."

"So you took something for it?" the S.N.O. said. "What did you take, nurse?"

"Aspirin."

"How many?"

"Two."

"Nothing else?"

"No, Miss Lewis."

The three other women stared at her. Extreme fear froze her limbs, but kept her brain alert. They had no proof and indeed how could they? She had not fiddled the doses from the ward supply for days now. Only... They must not suspend her. Not before she'd seen Zia again. Zia, her only hope.

For a few minutes no one spoke. Then the S.N.O. said, "You may go, Nurse Wilson."

She asked, with a carefully veiled insolence. "To Hunter Ward, Miss Lewis? I'm supposed to be on duty there in half an hour."

"I am aware of that. And that you have already had your breakfast. Two cups of black coffee and no food. Not a substantial provision for four hours of work."

Fear ran high again.

"Who told you — ?" she began, but the other held up a hand.

"You know perfectly well that I am not altogether satisfied with your explanation. But as far as Miss Hallet's death is concerned the various checks by the pharmacy and the medical staff have not shown any fault on the nursing side. It is up to you, Nurse Wilson, to prove we can trust you."

"Thank you for nothing," Moll said rudely as she flounced out of the room.

"I think she'll put the rope round her own neck," the S.N.O. said, which made the other two shudder, for it placed their elderly head in a generation that acknowledged evil in men and women and approved of retribution for crime, Capital retribution; the rope, in fact.

She noticed their reaction with a certain impatience. She laughed.

"You look shocked. I only meant if Nurse Wilson turns out to be a drug addict she'll have to go, for her own sake as much as the hospital's. Obviously Hallet's overdose was not Wilson's doing; she was more likely to take the post-operation doses herself. But fuddled heads are no good in a ward, far too dangerous." She paused, then gave her orders. "From now on, and that means tonight, she is not to have access to the dangerous drugs cupboard in Hunter. I have asked Nurse Biggs to have a word with me before she goes on duty."

Moll Wilson reached Hunter Ward a few minutes after eight that evening. She found Nurse Street stowing away the night nurses' dinner in the frig. Though the outside catering firm no longer used the fire escape to bring up their supplies, Tim always went down in the lift to guard against interference and secure their delivery past the pickets in the hall and on the third floor landing. Even Armstrong, the black porter, no longer dared to take the lift beyond that point.

Tim shut the door of the frig and said, "There you are, Moll. Luxury stew and ice cream." He straightened himself and went on, "Mr. Turner was in today to take out the Camplin's stitches. Quite a turn-up. She said he'd promised there'd be no scar and there were all these red lines. Old Turner treats her like a half-baked child. He just said the lines would turn white in time and when she said, 'But I cannot 'ave lines on my face,' he said 'At your age, Mrs. Camplin, it is natural to have some lines on the face. The result is very satisfactory.' "

Moll had to laugh in spite of her growing misery.

"Thanks a lot, Tim," she said. "Get along with you, now. I'll have a little word with poor old Camplin. When will she be going out?"

"End of next week, Turner said."

Moll waited, hiding her impatience, until he had left the ward. She expected Nurse Biggs to appear at any moment, but the ward was quiet and there were no messages on Sister's desk. It was too early for the bedpan round. She must see Camplin, must *must*! Tim's news made it natural, even if Biggs arrived in the next few minutes.

In the private room she began with easy confidence.

"So Mr. Turner has been today. Tim tells me he's very pleased with you."

Mrs. Camplin laughed harshly. Her face looked strangely different without dressings; her new, shortened, and narrowed nose no longer dominated the heavy jaw, but seemed to make the dark eyes above both huge and very menacing.

"And I am not pleased with myself," she said. "I do not look different, I look a caricature of myself."

This was so true that Moll was speechless.

"You have not come from sympathy, or from curiosity," the sufferer declared, "so I must tell you I have nothing any more for you. Nothing at all."

"But you said —"

"I told you where to go and I gave you money because I know you are always needing money, and never have any. So now that is ended. Finish. Caput."

"*Please*!" Moll's desperation was evident; so much so that Mrs. Camplin felt she must revise her former intention of having nothing more to do with this stupid little junky. She had better not push the girl to full confession; not while she herself was still tied to her bed here in bloody St. Edmunds Hospital. She found her purse.

"I can't..." the girl was babbling, "can't get through

tonight... Still on duty... They'll be watching... Just for tonight... Please. *Please*!"

"Be quiet!" Mrs. Camplin said sharply. "You whine like a peasant. Open my locker. The bottom drawer. That box. Under the jewel tray. Worthless copies, so don't try again to steal —"

"I never!" Moll panted.

"Take what you must." To herself she affirmed there would be only this woman's prints on the box and its contents. "Now go. I prefer Nurse Biggs shall settle me for the night. She has worked in my country. She understands how the washing must be done."

Moll stowed away her temporary salvation in the pocket of her uniform and went across the corridor to Mrs. Mitchell's room. The old lady was up, dressed, sitting in her armchair and chatting merrily with Miss Norris, the V.A.D. who had just finished making her bed.

"Not undressed yet, Mrs. Mitchell," she exclaimed.

"No hurry, dear," Miss Norris said. "I'm just about to give her a hand."

"It's high time you were off," Moll said.

"Don't discourage her," Mrs. Mitchell protested. "With Miss Norris and Mrs. Armstrong, bless their hearts, I'm getting more attention even than I had last year."

Moll left the room. Mr. Graham was O.K. Tim would have seen to him and he'd be out in another couple of days. Miss Field, the secretary, was leaving tomorrow. Her employer had lost the battle with the telephone operators; he could get no messages through to her now, so he was moving her to a private nursing home the next day. After all, the tests for which she had come in were all negative. There was nothing to keep her here and the rest and reassurance had already done her as much good as her timid, difficult temperament would allow. Or so Dr. Thompson's written comment had put in her notes. Moll wondered why her boss thought so much of her. Clever, highly efficient, his memory, his right hand aid, or just his floozy, valued simply for her palely pretty face?

The ward corridor was still deserted, still quiet. Moll went into the lavatory to give herself the rescue dose Mrs. Camplin had allowed her. When she reached the ward again she found that Nurse Biggs had arrived and was looking for her. They met in the ward kitchen.

"I have just been speaking to the S.N.O.," the latter told her. "She sent for me. I didn't go to her." This because Moll's dark eyes had accused her fiercely. "No, don't say anything. She's on the warpath: she's up here now, speaking to the pay-beds. She's with Mrs. Camplin at the moment."

Moll breathed, "Oh, my God!" and turned away, feeling sickness sweep over her. She leaned on the kitchen sink and felt Nurse Biggs's kind arm steadying her. "What did she say about me?" she moaned, careless of what the agency nurse might conclude from that.

"Nothing much. It was mostly to put me in complete charge of tonight's treatment up here. No real reason. Except she means to take you off night duty from tomorrow and get Dr. Thompson to see you and perhaps he'll advise a holiday or something before you go on day work."

Moll did not answer. It was, perhaps, less than she had been waiting to hear even an hour ago, since she had slammed the door of the head nurse's office behind her. But it was no less deadly for the lack of drama. It was the end for her and she knew it.

Accepting that conclusion as final, inevitable, she went about her immediate duties quietly and efficiently. She took temperatures, she counted pulses. Though she administered no sleep-inducing drugs, she straightened bedclothes, provided bedpans, collected and moved away flowers from locker tops, listened to chatter from those patients who found the 'lights out' hour of nine o'clock unnaturally early.

Among these last was Lionel Cox in Bed 5, directly opposite Miss Adams, the school teacher. When Moll turned from him to go he caught her by her bare forearm and pulled her back.

"I want to talk to you, nurse," he pleaded.

"It's your bedtime. Don't you go to bed at nine at home?"

"No fear."

"Watching tele?"

"Ya. Or down at the club, I was in the gym class as a nipper. Not after this started. No point now."

His voice, wavering between high and low, rose and broke on the last words. Moll stood, anchored by his hand, unable to find denial, which would be totally untrue, or comfort, equally dishonest.

"Sit down," Lionel said. "I want to talk to you. *You* don't ever tell me I must keep cheerful, keep hoping."

"There's no harm in that," Moll said feebly.

"There's no bloody point in it," the boy said violently. "As if I didn't know what it is. I've heard it said dozens of times — leukaemia — no cure, just a question of time."

She had sat down on the side of his bed where he had moved to give her room, patting the place with the hand he took from her arm.

"This new treatment does work," she insisted.

"They're finding out more all the time. If it hadn't been —" She checked herself, appalled by what she had so nearly said.

"If it hadn't been available when I was first brought in here, I'd be dead now. Was that what you were going to say?"

She nodded and he saw in the dim blue light from over his bed that her eyes had filled with tears.

"I wish it hadn't!" he burst out furiously. "I wish I'd gone before I really knew, as I do now. All the things I'll never do, never see! Just a darned guinea-pig waiting and waiting."

"And hoping, Lionel," said Nurse Biggs' firm voice as she came into the cubicle. "Everyone's trying their very best to help *you*, Lionel Cox, not just a guinea-pig. You must help *them* with your own courage and refusal to be beat."

"Phooey!" said Lionel. He turned on his side and shut his eyes and lay still. The two nurses left the cubicle together.

"Try to rest, Moll," Nurse Biggs said as they reached the end of the ward together. It was the first time she had used the other's Christian name. She saw how frantically disturbed the girl was. Her body was trembling, her hands twisting together. "I'll take the desk in the ward if you like. I don't suppose there'll be any emergencies. Mr. Gates is a good deal better, isn't he?"

"That's because they've told him he hasn't got lung cancer — yet," Moll answered. "But he still smokes like a chimney. His lungs are pretty rotten, Dr. Thompson told Sister."

"Why don't you have a rest in Sister's room?" Nurse Biggs went on. "You look as if you needed it."

She expected an outburst of anger, at least a bitter protest, but got neither.

"Later," Moll said, quite sensibly. The trembling had left her though her face showed her misery. "I'll get our dinner a bit early tonight, if you don't mind. And I think I will sit down for a bit. Do you mind if I just go back to my room for my library book? I'm due to give it in tomorrow and I want to finish it."

"Of course," Nurse Biggs said, pleased to find so much reasonable agreement.

Moll was away from the ward for about twenty minutes and Nurse Biggs took advantage of her absence to check the contents of the drug cupboards, with the pharmacist's list, after which she locked them up again. She had just finished this task when the other nurse came back.

"Got your book?" Nurse Biggs asked, seeing no likely volume in the girl's hand.

"It's in Sister's room. Anything doing?"

"Nothing so far."

A bell sounded.

"There now! Daphne, of course. I'll see what she wants."

Moll hurried away up the ward, moving briskly, quite herself again. As she disappeared behind the curtains Nurse Biggs went quickly into Sister Baker's room. Nurse Wilson's handbag was on the desk, but no book, library or otherwise. She was back in her chair in the ward when Moll joined her.

"Well?" Nurse Biggs asked.

"Pain in her right arm above the elbow. Tender, too. She moaned when I touched it, — barely touched it. I must say there seems to be a bit of swelling there, perhaps redness, but I didn't use a torch."

Nurse Biggs frowned.

"Like her to spring something quite new on us," she said. "I know these hysterics. She hasn't been scratching herself or putting an irritant on the arm or something, has she? They'll go to all lengths to attract attention."

"Not as far as I know," Moll answered. "I didn't ask any questions. She's fairly dopey, so I just told her to go to sleep and forget about it and it would be O.K. in the morning."

"Let's hope so," Nurse Biggs told her. "What with the coroner's officer coming tomorrow to take our stories about Hallet —"

"The police!" Moll gasped. "That's a policeman, isn't it? The coroner's officer?"

Nurse Biggs nodded.

"He has to get particulars, statements, I suppose, for the inquest. Now all the tests are through. We all know it was an overdose, but nobody seems to have found out which department slipped up and how."

"I'm hungry," said Nurse Wilson. "How about you?"

"It's barely eleven."

"It'll be half-past by the time I've warmed up our dinner. I didn't feel like eating for breakfast. I'm hungry."

"Then I'll just slip along to Bed 3," Nurse Biggs said, getting up from her chair. As she moved along the corridor she said to herself, "She didn't fetch her book. She went to get a fix. But she'll deny it if I say I might report her. She's desperate. I think she's desperate."

Daphne Parker was asleep; Nurse Biggs crept away again. She peeped in at the others; all asleep, or pretending to be so. Mrs. Hurst, the local mayor's mother-in-law, was snoring. Nurse Biggs moved her sideways to free her throat of the obstructing tongue; the effect was successful, but temporary.

After the meal the two women settled down again as before. Nurse Biggs had an evening paper with her to keep her awake if there was no work to be done. But she anticipated further trouble with Daphne Parker and that kept her alert. As did her continuing and growing anxiety over Moll Wilson. The girl had said she was hungry but she had eaten very little. Quite obviously she had forced herself to swallow food and keep it down. Nurse Biggs prayed she might be sick which would give her sufficient excuse to call the Night Sister and report her colleague too ill to continue.

But Moll controlled herself, for she had reached that point of no return she had foreseen several times of late and knew now was reached. Lionel's lament still rang in her mind. Why had he not gone before he knew his fate? Why keep him now that he did know it? Why keep going herself when she knew her own inevitable end? However many times they brought her back, that end would still lie before her.

There had been ecstasy at first, greater than the following hell. Now it was all hell, because fear had taken the place of ecstasy and was with her morning and night, awake or asleep.

And the unexpected withdrawal of Mrs. Camplin's marvellous support, generosity, kindness. A different Mrs. Camplin today, another cause of fear. And the police tomorrow. There must be no tomorrow.

Daphne's arm continued to give trouble. Nurse Biggs's attention was concentrated upon discovering the cause, still not at all recognisable. She tried hot packs and mild pain killers. If the telephone had been working she would have summoned the houseman. But Nurse

Wilson was very drowsy, poor thing, quite useless as a messenger or a nurse. Night Sister's visit was due, so Nurse Biggs continued her ministrations until her superior's arrival about half an hour later.

This produced a result that put the difficult hysteric's complaint in the shade for several hours. Sister, highly indignant at the state of affairs in Hunter Ward, marched into Sister Baker's room to hand out a first-class rocket to the suspected drug addict. She found Moll Wilson collapsed over the desk with her head resting on a sealed envelope addressed to 'The Coroner in charge of the inquest on Sister Hallet'. The erring nurse was deeply unconscious, barely breathing, with a feeble, but still recognisable, pulse.

From the ward below, Night Sister put emergency measures into action, and to this the lay staff responded at once with full co-operation. In fact most of those involved showed how thankful they were to work normally again for a spell.

But all to no purpose. The drugs Moll had secured with Mrs. Camplin's money, in her brief absence from the ward that night, were enough to kill six normal people. The hospital worked on her all the following day, but she died the next evening without recovering consciousness.

8

THOUGH MRS. CAMPLIN had seemed to agree with Mr. Turner that her stay in hospital need not last very much longer and he had promised to discharge her at the end of the week, after one final examination, she had continued to follow the very private time-table she had arranged for herself before she had even entered St. Edmunds for her operation.

Her visitors, who came daily, were all expected: they followed the given plan, reporting the news they were sent to give her. Experienced as she was, she had not failed to grasp the equally wide experience of Nurse Biggs, including the latter's knowledge of eastern languages. She had tested this conclusion with a few phrases, spoken jocularly, which had amused them both. She had then gone on to try the more western Mediterranean tongues. Here she found to her surprise that Nurse Biggs was as deficient in Greek, Italian, Spanish and French, and she was proficient in Arabic, Turkish, Hindi and Urdu.

However, most of her visitors could understand French, though the replies were halting. So Nurse Biggs, who had looked forward nostalgically to brushing up her former fluency, was astonished to hear a language she recognised as French, without understanding a word of the conversation.

The news of Nurse Wilson's death came to Mrs. Camplin from the V.A.D., Miss Norris, who brought her the special mid-morning small cup of black Turkish coffee for which the patient had provided the unground beans and a small electric grinder.

"Have they told you we've had another accident?" Miss Norris asked, blinking her watery little eyes as she always did when she was confused or upset.

"Why, no," said Mrs. Camplin, alert at once. "To one of us?"

She meant the patients, the paying ones, for she was barely conscious of any other kind in the ward.

"No. Nurse Wilson. Unconscious and not expected to live."

Getting no response from Mrs. Camplin, she added, "The night nurse. The young one. They all call her Moll. Always first names now. Surnames in my childhood. Not the agency nurse. That's Miss Biggs."

"Yes, yes." Mrs. Camplin was thinking rapidly, trying not to panic, trying to plan carefully. "Yes, yes, I know who you mean. I have thought she was not well since I came here. Too pale. Too much worry. You all work so hard."

Sister Baker's arrival prevented any further discussion. Miss Norris scuttled away to chatter her news to Mrs. Mitchell. Mrs. Camplin lay back on her pillows waiting for Sister to deliver whatever it was that had brought her.

It was nothing of much importance, just a message from Mr. Turner to say he would not be able to come down to St. Edmunds as promised, but he would be delighted to see her at his consulting rooms in the West End on the day and at the time she was expecting to see him in Hunter Ward.

"Would that be possible?" Sister asked, trying to hide her rising hope that Mrs. Camplin would now discharge herself.

Mrs. Camplin understood this. Mr. Turner's suggestion suited her admirably and she rejoiced that such a reasonable excuse had been presented to her on a plate, as it were. What silly expressions these English used! But she was inclined to tease solemn, disapproving Sister Baker a little, so she said, "It is a shock, but I have no choice, have I? I must leave, but it will not be such a great hardship, with your confusion in the service departments, as you call them."

Sister Baker said nothing, only waited to get a definite answer. This also Mrs. Camplin guessed and gave up the unequal game. When the opponent refuses to play, refuses to get excited, refuses even to speak...!

"I will talk to my sister or it may be my brother-in-law tonight. I am quite well, it is just the scars, still so ugly, so red. I will wear the dress I am expected to wear when I shop at home. Tomorrow; if it can be arranged."

"Will you telephone Mr. Turner about your appointment at his consulting room or would you like me to do that for you?"

"You are so kind, Sister. Please, yes. I will go to Harley Street at the time he says. That is where I saw him the first time."

So the next morning, soon after nine o'clock she left her expensive cubicle, attended by two gentlemen each wearing a long black coat and a fez and clad herself, over her western suit, in a voluminous black djellabia flowing from head to foot, with a couple of narrow slits ıor her nose and mouth and two holes through which her dark eyes peered without expression.

"Well, Mrs. Camplin, no one can see your scars now," Sister told her, offering her hand to shake, but finding no response from the depths of the black robe.

"I am grateful," Mrs. Camplin said. "You have been very good in spite of the dreadful conditions. Yes, you have done your best."

Sister Baker wanted to say, "Ungrateful bitch! Go to hell, scars and all!" but she smiled professionally and watched Armstrong load the four suitcases and the three passengers into the lift he had brought to the top floor for them, encouraged by the ten-pound note one of the passengers had slipped to him when Porter Wells was stuck with the telephone.

A taxicab drove the three to an embassy in Mayfair, where they all got out. They stood on the bottom step of the front entrance, chatting, until the cab turned away round the corner, then they walked off in the opposite direction. At a cross roads one of the gentlemen took an eastern farewell of Mrs. Camplin while her other escort signalled a fresh taxi. In this the two of them drove to north London in the neighbourhood of Barnet. Here they got out midway along a row of late Victorian houses set a little back from the road and half hidden by overgrown laurels in the small front gardens. Again they waited for the taxi to turn round and drive away towards Golders Green before they rang the bell of one of these houses and were admitted immediately.

At St. Edmunds the loss of the exotic but tiresome Mrs. Camplin caused nothing but relief and satisfaction. As Mr. Graham said to Patty Shaw, "Surely now we've lost the rich foreigner and the tycoon's pet and you'll see the last of me the day after tomorrow, there won't be any excuse for the bastards downstairs to persist in their bloody-mindedness?"

Patty laughed.

"There'll only be Mrs. Mitchell and she's been coming in every year for ages."

"The hardy perennial, eh? Never really ill, but means to make the most of her premium to B.U.P.A. or is it one of the other clubs?"

"I don't really know, Mr. Graham," Patty said, giving place to Tim Street, who was wheeling in a trolley. "But it's great we've had the last of Mrs. C. and her bell."

In this she was less than correct; Hunter Ward had not heard the last of Mrs. Camplin. For the post-mortem on Nurse Wilson had disclosed what several people, doctors and nurses, had begun to suspect. Her body gave evidence of addiction to the so-called 'hard' drugs and in the search for the source of material several points of interest emerged. She appeared to have no stocks hidden in Hunter Ward or in her room at the Nurses Home, which stood in the grounds of the hospital. In the careful search at the latter place a dog trained for the purpose was set on to nose out the expected hiding place, but with no success.

"The hospital ward then," suggested the handler.

Here an unexpected but very positive result was their reward. In Mrs. Camplin's room, not yet cleaned, nor even the used bed linen collected, the dog announced his find, indicating in no uncertain manner that the bottom drawer in the locker beside the bed, though now empty, had recently held what they were looking for.

The coroner's officer, who had gone to Hunter Ward with the dog handler, now decided that the case of Nurse Wilson, query suicide, was probably linked to that of Sister Hallet, query careless accident. And whereas the source and actual cause of both deaths was the same, a fresh, disgraceful link with Mrs. Camplin was possible, even probable.

So, having sealed the door of Private Room 1, and warned Sister Baker, the Law retreated, with the dog, and it was not many hours before a Detective Inspector Holmes climbed the stairs from the third floor to Hunter Ward.

To everyone's surprise, and this included all the remaining patients, the consultants, registrars and housemen, the nurses, the auxiliaries and Mrs. Armstrong, Inspector Holmes was not concerned with the interesting deaths of Sister Hallet and Nurse Wilson, but solely with Mrs. Camplin. Nor did he explain his particular interest in the only private patient who had paid all her own fees by the cheque of one of the best-known of British banks. He simply wanted to know all they could tell him about her case, her behaviour, the visitors who had brought her flowers and especially parcels. Also her attitude towards the younger staff and the nurses.

"She was not very popular with my nurses," Sister Baker said, "particularly since we started this trouble with the non-medical staff."

"Sort of politically-motivated strike," commented the Inspector.

"You can call it that if you like," Sister answered. "Most of us have stronger names for it and its leader, our head porter. You should ask the trade union official in Bed 3. Not much solidarity there."

Inspector Holmes changed the subject.

"You will have seen Mrs. Camplin when she came in," he said. "Can you describe her to me?"

Sister's description was a lame one, spoilt by her

trained reticence and unshakable loyalty to the nursing staff. If the Law wanted a description of Mrs. Camplin's cosmetic operation he must get it from the surgeon, Mr. Turner. She did not say so aloud, but Holmes understood her. He asked if any of the Nurses could help him with more detail.

"Poor Nurse Wilson might have done so; she was quite a friend, never would listen to a word against her, said she was the most generous, kind, understanding, patient, brave... A marvel, in every way!"

Sister stopped, for she realised suddenly where this eulogy, ascribed to the dead nurse, was leading. Inevitably. Incriminatingly.

"Well, yes," the Detective Inspector said gently. "You will have guessed, of course, that Nurse Wilson's praise was a part of her — well, gratitude to Mrs. Camplin, misplaced as it was?"

"Yes," said Sister Baker, clearly upset. "But all that will have to come out at the inquest, won't it? I don't want...I didn't mean..." She broke off, then said, bitterly, "You know something about Mrs. Camplin you haven't told me! Are you saying with that sniffing dog and all, the woman is a known drug-pusher? And helped poor Moll Wilson to kill herself?"

"I'm not saying anything at present," said the Inspector, "and I must ask you not to spread these conclusions around the hospital."

"I think you'll find most of them are circulating already," Sister told him.

Detective Inspector Holmes dealt very lightly with the rest of the nursing staff, reserving until later in the day an interview with Nurse Biggs, since she was in bed and not due to appear until eight o'clock that evening.

Of the patients Mrs. Mitchell could speak clearly

about the large number of visits Mrs. Camplin had received from friends and the several kinds of 'foreign jabber' as she called it, heard faintly through two layers of plywood, the walls of her own and Mrs. Camplin's rooms.

Mr. Graham said he had been fully aware of Nurse Wilson's failing but had not considered it any of his business to point it out to Sister. The girl had been quite capable of looking after him until the night of her death, when Nurse Biggs had attended to him instead. He did not point out that he had not at any time accepted hypodermic injections from Moll.

No one else among the patients had anything at all to say about Mrs. Camplin.

So Detective Inspector Holmes left Hunter Ward and walked down the stairs, all the way down, to the junior medical staff common room, where he had arranged to see the surgical houseman who had been present at Mrs. Camplin's operation, the anaesthetist who had given the anaesthetic and Guy Harper who had assisted Mr. Turner.

To each of these in turn he showed a series of photographs. They were all of the same size, a full face and a profile on the same sheet, numbered, but not named. They were all of women, dark-haired, dark-eyed, dusky skinned, with large, prominent, beaky noses and wide, full-lipped mouths.

The doctors stared at them in silence; the houseman then threw out a ribald remark, capped by the anaesthetist. Each declared he had never seen any of them in his life.

But Guy continued to look them over, turning from one to the other, laying aside those he had finally discarded. He reduced the number from six to two, then looked up at Holmes.

"Could be either of these," he said. "We're supposed to match them with Mrs. Camplin, are we? *Before* her op.?"

"Exactly."

"Why?" the anaesthetist asked.

Before Holmes could answer Guy said, "It's obvious, isn't it? They think Mrs. Camplin was pushing the drugs and it seems they want to match her, in her real name, with one of these known baddies. Isn't that so?" he asked the Inspector.

"Something like it. I'm asking you three if you recognise her in any of these photos."

The houseman said he'd only seen her when he helped to move her to the theatre and back and she was flat out both ways with her face covered up in dressings of one kind or another.

The anaesthetist said he hadn't looked at her face at all. His sole concern had been to administer the appropriate anaesthetic and maintain it while giving the surgeon full freedom of access to the operation area.

Guy said, "Can't Mr. Turner help you? He saw her in consultation twice, I think, before she came in. And he would have his own photograph of her face."

"Only the nose," Inspector Holmes announced. "Not much help. Before operation —"

"I know," Guy interrupted. "That album he has. Before and After. She discharged herself today, ahead of time, but she was due to leave here the day after tomorrow and see him at his consulting room on Friday. He'll take the After photo then."

If she's still in the country, Holmes said to himself, but he made a note of the date.

"I think one of these might be her," Guy said,

handing back the two prints he had kept in front of him. Then he jumped up.

"Half a mo," he said. "I was forgetting. I wanted to keep a record myself, so I took a snap of her face as she lay on the trolley, just before Turner got going. Bandages off. The great man didn't object. He was flattered."

"You did *what?*" the Inspector shouted.

"Took a snap of her face. I haven't developed it yet. Haven't had time. I was in a hurry then because Turner wanted to get going."

"But I thought you were assisting. They told me —"

"Not really. He brought his own pet assistant to scrub up. I was background interest only. He doesn't belong to St. Edmunds. Condescended to operate here because she'd wangled the bed in Hunter and was in a hurry."

Seeing the mixture of relief, interest and impatience in Inspector Holmes's face Guy said, defensively, "The film's only half used. You'll have to give me a new one and save me the early pictures on it if you take it off me."

"Go and fetch your camera," Holmes said in a quiet, controlled voice. "No, I'll come with you. This may be a great help." He wanted to add, 'if you haven't wasted too much of my time already'.

In the police car on their way to his flat, Guy said, "She won't look like my photo now. Not by a long chalk. Alters the face a lot mucking about with the nose. She'll have the scars showing still, though. Recent, of course."

"I'm aware of all that," the Inspector said patiently. "I'll see you get your camera and the early pictures back tomorrow."

9

THE CORONER WAS puzzled. Two deaths had taken place in the same ward at St. Edmunds Hospital, one a patient, the other a nurse and each from an overdose of narcotic drugs. Moreover the ward had been and still was subject to industrial action, 'politically motivated', as newspaper jargon had it. So the public's attention and interest in the two cases had been given a prominence they might otherwise have avoided. Inquests must be held, of course, but information was sadly lacking.

The coroner, through his officer, called for a statement of discovered facts and wanted to know when they would be ready and who would present them. Clearly the case must be taken with a jury.

Detective Inspector Holmes went to see him.

"It's like this," the coroner told him. "According to my officer information from the hospital, the ward record of dangerous drugs, issued and used, corresponds exactly with the prescriptions ordered and initialled by the doctors. The Sister in charge of Hunter Ward is certain that no mistake was made there. The hospital head pharmacist, who has been doing all the dispensing for the ward personally since the lay staff strike began, is in an excellent position to confirm this."

"So we can conclude," Inspector Holmes said firmly, "that the surplus dose given Miss Hallet and the fatal dose taken by Nurse Wilson came from some outside source."

"I suppose so," said the coroner. "Are you saying in other words that both deaths may have been brought about deliberately?"

The Inspector smiled.

"Isn't that rather jumping the gun?" he said. "I wouldn't go further than suggesting if carelessness came into the Hallet case, there must have been an extra supply of drugs *available in Hunter Ward.*"

"And you think there was?"

"I know there was."

"You can prove this?"

"I have proved it, up to a point."

"What point?"

"The point at which the provider, or pusher, if you like, left St. Edmunds and travelled to a house in Barnet, now being watched. Ports and air terminals have been alerted, but there are far too many open spaces, even fields, reasonably near Barnet, open to all comers, such as private helicopters. We can't put tabs on every exit point. Besides, we were not warned until after the nurse's death. In respect of this line of investigation, I mean."

"I have her letter, of course," said the coroner. "It isn't very explicit. Suggests her decision to kill herself, but not a word about where she got her supplies. Only confesses her addiction and accuses Miss Hallet of making her life unbearable. Absurd, really. The poor old woman was only in hospital two days altogether. Miss Wilson had never seen her before."

Detective Inspector Holmes nodded but did not say any more. The inquest on Sister Hallet would have to be opened and adjourned. Also on Nurse Wilson, a much simpler case in view of the letter and the evidence of access to supplies of the drugs. If he could find Mrs. Camplin, so much the better.

But he was not hopeful of success. All too likely she was out of the country by now. But it was worth going over Hunter Ward again in case he had missed clear evidence of the girl's addiction earlier than these last few weeks and her means of gratifying it before the appearance of the criminal Mrs. Camplin. He had concentrated so far on the doctors in order to avoid an excess of publicity the wretched hospital could well do without. Now it must be the turn once more of the patients and the nursing staff.

He heard from Patty Shaw a full account of her conversation with Sister Hallet while she was going through the routine preparations for the old woman's operation.

"She warned you off young doctors, did she? Well, that wasn't bad advice," he remarked.

"I didn't ask for it. Not that it worried me. Rather pathetic, really. No, the point was it was our Dr. Thompson."

"The consultant? But he isn't a young doctor, Miss Shaw."

She answered patiently, "He was a young doctor at the time old Hallet was talking about. Twenty years ago; she said so. Didn't know he'd come back to St. Edmunds. Not that a little thing like that would rock her. Old devil. It got about, too. Other people heard her."

Inspector Holmes moved on. Nurse Street had nothing to tell him. Sister Baker confirmed Patty's story and enlarged upon Sister Hallet's unappealing ways. She also disclosed her personal fears and suspicions about Nurse Wilson. She had hesitated to report the girl earlier than she did, chiefly because she had no direct evidence and partly because they were so pressed for time, and so overworked by the strike ban on the ward. It could be that, not the drugs, had driven Moll to take her life.

Moving on to the patients, Holmes found there had been no doubt in Mr. Graham's mind. As he pointed out to the Inspector he had travelled to many ports all over the world, he had been in contact with crews of many nationalities on the ships in which he had served. He knew a junky when he saw one. He had made an excuse to refuse any injection or tablet she had offered him. He knew his immediate post-operative treatment had been given him by the houseman while he was still half unconscious. And really there had been very little pain. It wasn't much of an operation, was it?

"I wouldn't know," Inspector Holmes said, shuddder-ing slightly. He was used to the thought, sometimes the experience of violence, even with knives to it. But imagining these cold-blood affairs, done on a helpless, unconscious victim, gave him the pip.

Most of the other patients had nothing at all to offer. Daphne Parker confirmed Patty's story, as did Miss Adams, the school teacher. Daphne also disclosed a queer exchange between Nurse Wilson and Sister Hallet on the evening of the day before the operations, her own as well as the retired Sister's.

"What was that?" Holmes asked. "Something else you heard?"

"Yes. Miss Hallet was criticising Moll, as we all called her, poor girl. Kindness itself, I must say, in spite of her failing. Something about Moll's eyes. Miss Hallet flashed a pocket torch at her. I saw it through the curtains and she said something about her, Moll's, pupils. Pins or something. Nutty, it sounded to me."

"Would it have been pin-point?" the Inspector asked carefully.

"Yes. I do believe it was! Did it mean anything? Really?"

"It might have."

He left Miss Parker's cubicle as soon as he could get away. There was only one more character he wanted to see and that was Nurse Biggs. On two counts. She might give him something useful on Mrs. Camplin and she had worked two night shifts with Moll Wilson.

But Nurse Biggs could tell him very little about Mrs. Camplin he did not already know. Except that in their slight exchanges in Arabic Nurse Biggs found her accent faintly unfamiliar, but the patient had not responded to the nurse's overtures in any other eastern language of the four she knew, though she had laughed on hearing the nurse's attempts at them.

"She certainly gave up her Arabic in talking to her visitors. Directly after she knew how much I understood."

"So what then?"

"French. Or I think it was French. I didn't rumble anything they said. Not a whole sentence. Only 'oui' and 'non'. These were the one or two late evening visitors; special concession to private patients."

None of this had any importance, Holmes decided. But Nurse Biggs had plenty to say about Moll Wilson and all of it was relevant, including the last words it appeared were said by Sister Hallet to anyone.

"You say you were issuing medicine, sleeping pills and so on to the medical patients and you were in cubicle 3 when you heard the deceased speak?"

"That's right, Inspector. Just before midnight. Nurse Wilson said she would attend to the surgical cases."

Holmes remembered that Mr. Graham refused to take drugs in any form from Nurse Wilson.

"What did you hear?"

"Sister Hallet said, 'Up to your tricks again, are you?' or something like that."

"How like?"

Nurse Biggs flushed.

"I think those were the words. Her voice was loud and harsh, or had been the night before. This was after the operation, so the voice was weaker, but still quite unmistakable."

"Did Nurse Wilson make any answer to this accusation?"

"Yes. She whispered a denial. She was trying to keep the conversation down, so as not to disturb the patients in the other curtained cubicles. And I was two beds away in Number 3."

"And they were in Number 1. What happened next?"

"Oh, I heard her go into Number 2, Miss Parker. The girl was too drowsy to say anything. She did just moan a little, I suppose when the needle went in, but Nurse Wilson didn't speak to her, only made a soothing noise."

"You were in cubicle 3 for some time?"

"Yes. The patient there is a chest case, medical. He was very distressed that night. Cough and difficulty in breathing."

"When you left him, where did you find Nurse Wilson?"

"In the ward kitchen, getting our dinner ready."

"Dinner? Oh yes, don't tell me. Midnight. Night duty. Right?"

"Quite right." Nurse Biggs beamed at him.

"Did she seem normal?"

"She did, then. It was later, when Daphne, Miss Parker, had her nightmare, I found Nurse Wilson asleep at the night nurse's desk in the ward. I stopped Daphne's hysterics and then I went to see if Sister Hallet had been upset by the noise and I found she was dead. So I waited for Night Sister to come on her round. I didn't dare leave the ward with Nurse Wilson like that, and the telephone wasn't working —"

"I know," Det. Inspector Holmes said. He had already interviewed Night Sister. Her account fitted Nurse Biggs's exactly. The question of Sister Hallet's overdose and Nurse Wilson's suicide began to take a very sinister and complementary meaning. Drugs were his line. He thought this double problem might well be shifted on to a different, a higher, level of crime, positive crime.

Meanwhile the situation in the hospital was unchanged; Hunter Ward was still 'blacked', though now, ten days from the start of the trouble, there was only one fee-paying patient left there, Mrs. Mitchell.

Mrs. Camplin, discharging herself on Wednesday, had been preceded by Miss Field, the personal secretary of her wealthy employer, who was insured by him for care and treatment. In spite of the fact that she had come in for total rest while her chronic indigestion was investigated, he had expected her to continue her former advisory work by telephone. When this service was held up, he whisked her away to a private nursing home. After all, the tests were all negative.

"The poor stooge never will get that complete rest old Thompson ordered," Trevor Leigh, the medical registrar, said to Guy Harper. "Will her boss's insurance run to this new move, I wonder?"

"Search me," said Guy. The intricacies of insurance, together with the zanier political moves of the N.H.S. were beyond him. He had no time for such things in his twenty-four-hour day in a seven-day week.

A few days later Mr. Graham had followed these two. He would have a fortnight at home before his ship sailed, instead of the single week he had expected. He looked forward to that, seeing more of the kids and having a more varied diet. His wife was a wizard cook.

"You're fine," Mr. Campbell told him. "But no golf, no moving furniture, and no fun and games in bed."

"Pity," said Mr. Graham gently, "seeing I'm away from home so much. But I expect you're right."

There were now in Hunter Ward three out of four empty wooden cubicles and two out of eight empty curtained beds. Bed 8 had never been filled, nor had Bed 1 after Miss Hallet's death. Soon there would be two more empty beds there. Miss Adams was leaving in three days' time to go to her married sister until her face was more presentable. Her resignation from her school had been accepted. She would apply for compensation before trying to get another teaching job. The spirit of greed, of refusal to serve others, of arrogance, of aggression, had begun to infect her, too, rising like an evil miasma through the wards of the hospital. She was a turned worm, she was a new rebel, she was in grave danger of losing both her vocation and her professional pride.

The same infection was beginning to appear in Miss Clark, the social services official in Bed 7. Dr. Thompson had already advised her that she was now quite physically fit to go back to work, but the prospect appalled her. How could she tackle unco-operative parents, particularly fathers, if they were liable to treat their young, defenceless children with the same total lack of responsibility, human kindness, and restraint shown by these hospital public employees? On the other hand, she was not enjoying her stay in St. Edmunds. She agreed with Dr. Thompson. She decided to find a small convalescent home on the south coast. The hospital Social Service Officer, formerly called Almoner, could help her. The sooner the better.

None of these problems disturbed Porter Wells, though the consultants took care to tell him of them, stressing the circumstances of the patients who were suffering from this unofficial, though Government-approved, industrial action. But Wells, though he considered he could ignore the patients, saw his opportunity to boost his case in the matter of Mrs. Hurst, in Bed 6. For one thing she was a patient of Dr. Thompson, who had spoken to him so rudely and unfairly about Miss Clark and the little secretary in the pay-bed, Miss Field. There could be no possible reason for old Mrs. Hurst to be in an amenity bed, except that she happened to be the mother-in-law of the local mayor, now in his second term of office, highly respected and liked and holding political views the exact opposite of those of Mr. Wells.

Mayor Ollershaw was perfectly aware of the regrettable goings-on at St. Edmunds. His borough on the whole was apathetic, a largely suburban, commuting, reasonably healthy population with a very mixed, multi-racial set of tenants in the council estates to the east and north of the former small country town. But the hospital was now news and this had brought the usual flood of journalists and photographers. Porter Wells had been much gratified by the attentions of these people, who had found him far better value from the story angle than the consultants, with their brief, cold, disturbing facts and blank faces.

The mayor expected to be met at the hospital by a barrage of newsmen as well as by a picket of strikers. He decided to brave them all in style: it was very ill-advised.

Wearing his chain of office, sitting in the back of his official Rolls-Royce, he was driven up to the front of the hospital, disembarked slowly, and proceeded up the entrance steps with his accustomed genial dignity.

The journalists were delighted. They took photographs, they asked questions, all of which he answered. They formed two columns, one on either side of him, they followed him into the main hall, where Wells and a number of colleagues waited, affronted, but not afraid.

Mr. Ollershaw marched up .to the lifts and waited. Nothing happened. One of the journalists stepped forward to press the call button, but thought better of it and stepped back. Mr. Wells moved towards the mayor. Though he had guessed correctly that the man had come to visit his mother-in-law in the 'black' ward, it was just possible his purpose was some other, perhaps, public one, so he asked, with a stony face, "Can I help you?"

"Yes, you can," Mr. Ollershaw said, breathing hard. "My wife's mother is a National Health patient with a National Health doctor and has been admitted to this amenity ward. I have come to see her and I demand the proper service I am entitled to as a ratepayer and tax payer."

"Services to fee-paying patients have been withdrawn," Wells answered, and added insolently, because the jeering faces of some of the journalists were upsetting him, "I should have thought you'd have heard of it by now."

"If you stop me visiting my relation I shall call the police," the mayor shouted.

"We're not stopping you," Wells told him. "The stairs are at the end of that corridor."

"The lifts go up to the third floor," one of the journalists called helpfully. "It's only one floor further to Hunter Ward."

"Then I'll take the lift up to the third floor," the mayor said.

"You bloody won't!" the porter yelled.

"Don't you dare speak to me like that, my man!"

"Get the hell out of this hospital!"

"One of you fetch the police," Mr. Ollershaw appealed to the audience.

But no one moved, no lift door opened, the mayor knew the support he had looked for was mere curiosity and that the longer this went on the more humiliation would be his. So, controlling his anger he pushed Wells out of his way with one powerful hand against his chest and strode off towards the staircase.

Porter Wells, purple in the face, broke into threats and curses, yelled it was assault and he'd have the bastard in court for it. But a photographer, making for the door, shouted back that he'd got a grand set of pictures of the whole scene for his paper and the others, following, went laughing and joking down the steps.

Mr. Ollershaw did not have to walk all the way up the stairs. At the first floor he came across an open service lift and stepping inside crouched down in one corner behind a loaded trolley. It went up to the third floor and since the porter who was working it was Armstrong, he ignored the unexpected visitor until the lift stopped at the third floor.

"Is this Hunter Ward?" Mr. Ollershaw asked then, rising to his feet.

"No, sir. This third floor. Next one up Hunter Ward."

"Then take me there. At once, please."

This was not the way to speak to him, Armstrong thought. He guessed the visitor was upset and why. He was impressed by the shining mayoral chain about the visitor's neck. But there was a limit to the amount of kindness he would deal out to the boss type, gold chains notwithstanding. Besides, Joe Wells had threatened his job more than once and he understood where the power lay in St. Edmunds Hospital just now. So he ignored the stranger and pulled the trolleys out to deliver them to the two wards on the third floor.

When he came back he found the mayor still standing in the lift.

"I go down, now, sir," he said politely. "You want for to go down?"

"Good God, no," Mr. Ollershaw cried, dashing out of the lift. "You're crazy!" he went on. "Stark, staring bonkers, the lot of you!"

But he climbed the stairs to Hunter Ward and there found a polite, concerned ward sister, but an only moderately sympathetic mother-in-law, who wanted to complain about the general lack of real comfort in the ward, instead of listening to his heroic success in reaching her bedside.

But there was no difficulty about his escape from the hospital. Tim Street and Patty Shaw decided that such an important witness to their plight must be given every encouragement to make the most of the disgraceful happenings at St. Edmunds. They consulted Sister Baker, who agreed.

So Tim went down to direct the Rolls to drive round to the rear of the wing and stop at the foot of the fire-escape. Patty opened the door on to the escape and led his worship down. He needed a good deal of soothing help, for he had a poor head for heights and had never before used a very long, very steep, totally openwork iron contraption, with a thin, cold, metal handrail, slightly roughened by rust. Mr. Ollershaw tottered down each angled section of this formidable descent, only kept from a stumbling fall by the sight of his mayoral car drawn up close to its foot, with his chauffeur's uplifted, astonished face marking his progress.

10

THOUGH HUNTER WARD was now reduced to one paying patient, old Mrs. Mitchell, one surgical case, Miss Parker and two medical ones, the boy Lionel and the union official, Mr. Gates, the unofficial action of the porters, telephonists, orderlies and kitchen staff continued. Their encounter with the mayor had brought them publicity of a very unwelcome kind, since the journalists, backed by several splendid photographs, had reduced the incident to farce.

True, Mrs. Hurst, doubly shocked by her son-in-law's plight and her own exposure to criticism, had left St. Edmunds for a nursing home in a neighbouring borough, more expensive than the statutory amenity bed. So far, this move had not been revealed to the Press.

The consultants, on the other hand, seeing no solution to the problem, no longer had any wish to fight for their contract rights. Working strictly within the terms of these contracts, would not alter the situation in Hunter Ward. Better far to arrange other means of treating their legitimate private patients, empty Hunter and arrange to fill it with a mixed lot from the waiting lists, who would probably object strongly to finding themselves in curtained or solid cubicles, men and women together in the ward, no continuous television, no unending intimate gossip.

So Sister Baker found the demands upon her considerably relaxed and did not much like it. However, there were still one or two problems to worry her, the most pressing being Daphne Parker.

It was on the day of the mayor's visit that Bob Frost came to her about Daphne.

"Have you seen that girl's arm?" he asked. "I mean lately?"

"No, Mr. Frost. Not for the last ten days. Why?"

"She complains of a lot of pain in the upper arm."

"She's done that ever since her operation. She really ought to have gone out by now, only Dr. Fisher isn't too happy about her mental condition."

"We hoped the appendicectomy would cure that."

"You can't cure hysteria."

Seeing the young houseman still waited, Sister said, "All right. Show me."

Miss Parker made a great show of painful difficulty in throwing off her fluffy bed jacket. She displayed her upper arm, turning her head away and wincing. "Well," said Sister and stared at Bob. For Daphne's arm was clearly swollen and very red. "Glands too?" she asked.

"Yes," said the houseman.

"Perhaps you've been lying on it," Sister said to Miss Parker. "I'll get Nurse Shaw to see to it."

Back in her own room she asked, "Is this the first time you've noticed anything wrong?"

"Well — yes. I've not actually —"

"Examined the arm before. Wolf, wolf, was it? I

wouldn't blame you. But you'd better get Mr. Harper up at once."

Guy came and started antibiotics. Next day Mr. Campbell examined the arm before his Out-patient session. He spoke to Sister.

"That girl's cooking an abscess. Upper arm. How the devil did she get that? In that position?"

"I'm sure I don't know," Sister answered indignantly. She hesitated, then went on. "Before we had antibiotics, when I was in the Guides, doing First-Aid courses and Nursing courses, we had impressed on us the danger of dirty needles and syringes for injections. There were none of these pre-sterilised jobs we have now. Everything then was boiled up and kept in spirit and washed out with sterilised water."

"Are you suggesting that Miss Parker could have been given a post-operative injection with a dirty syringe?"

"No. Not really. But it looks like... I've seen, years ago..."

"It's a thought, isn't it?" Campbell said frowning. "With all this upset over supplies, trolleys, the pharmacy — though Brentford says he's O.K. Well, Sister, let's hope the penicillin will do its stuff and we won't need more surgery."

They both shuddered. Miss Parker would be the worst kind of patient to take any slip in her treatment with understanding. Not to speak of her mother. And with the modern bias against the medical profession.

He was not the only one to worry. Dr. Joan Fisher had kept up her regular visits to Daphne, for she continued to be interested in the girl's progress. She, too, was horrified by the latest development. Having done her best to reassure Daphne, now frightened and tearful over this new obstacle to her discharge from the hospital, she went in search of David Thompson.

Their new relationship had had a very invigorating effect upon them both. Each was basically inclined to melancholy, with a gloomy view of the human race in general and themselves in particular. So the enchanting discovery of their mutual love was sharpening their wits as well as intoxicating their senses.

"Guy says Sister Baker thinks she's been given an injection with a dirty syringe as part of her immediately post-operative treatment. The question is why and by whom?"

David thought for a full minute before answering.

"Why," he said slowly, "could be because the doses given out had already been used."

"By Nurse Wilson," said Joan eagerly. "Because she'd given them to herself."

"Steady on. Haven't we already suggested Sister Hallet got some extra doses, meant for other patients, by mistake."

"Well, yes. Ian went through that angle with Inspector Holmes. Graham, the chap with the hernia, rumbled Moll Wilson's addiction and refused to let her give him any drugs, by injection or otherwise. Not that he ever needed anything at night, even on the first day."

"But I expect the usual was prescribed for him. So with Daphne's intended dose that would give Moll three doses to use on Hallet, instead of one. Which would do the trick, wouldn't it?"

"Surely,"

They stared at one another.

"You realise, of course," David said, "what you are suggesting? That Moll deliberately murdered Sister Hallet."

"What else can we suggest? She wasn't in her right mind, was she?"

"Perhaps not."

They went together to find Ian Campbell, but he was shut away in the operating theatre, so Joan left a note for him suggesting a meeting with herself and David, if possible before he left the hospital that day, otherwise tomorrow at any time he liked to fix. Meanwhile, at David's insistence, they both went back to Hunter Ward, to put their theory to Sister Baker.

At first she was very unwilling to discuss it.

"But Sister," Joan argued, "doesn't our theory fit with what actually happened to Sister Hallet and Daphne. An overdose in the old woman's body and this abscess from a dirty injection in the girl's arm? Poor kid, she did complain a lot about pain that first night. If her late night dose was only water we can't blame her, can we? And we just thought she was exaggerating as usual!"

"According to Nurse Biggs," Sister reminded them, "Nurse Wilson was under drugs that night. If she used the doses, all three of them, for Hallet, where did she get her own fix? Besides, Moll may have been an addict, but she was a good nurse for all that. Until recently, quite recently, I mean. Nurse Biggs agrees with me. You can ask her." She went on with emphasis, "No, Dr. Thompson, I'll never believe one of my nurses actually, deliberately, killed Miss Hallet. Nor gave a dirty injection to Miss Parker. Whoever did those two things, if that was indeed done, it must have been someone from outside the ward."

"Perhaps not someone from outside, who brought a syringe — an unsterilised syringe and filled it with tap water," said Dr. Thompson, annoyed by Sister's unreasonable defence of her junior colleagues. "But it could have been one of the patients."

To his surprise she was not upset by his intended levity. She simply answered, "I'm afraid Miss Hallet had a lot of enemies. She spent her life insulting and wounding people. In all walks of life," she added, looking him straight in the eye.

Joan quickly brought the discussion to an end.

"Wasn't that a bit obvious?" David grumbled, as they left the ward.

"Yes, darling. But we weren't getting anywhere, were we? It occurs to me our idea doesn't work, unless we know that Moll had an outside source of her drug and the money to pay for it. When you said, 'Or one of the patients' I thought of the exotic Mrs. Camplin and her spectacular exit, veiled and guarded in very eastern fashion."

"Of course. Inspector Holmes had a long session with her, didn't he?"

Later that day when they explained their theory once more to Ian Campbell, he was able to tell them that the detective had already linked Mrs. Camplin with the nurse's death. Investigations were continuing, he had been told. When the inquest on Miss Wilson had been adjourned, further search would be made.

The full meaning of this very vague piece of non-information did in fact appear at the inquest. For the first time Moll's last letter, addressed to the coroner and which he had read, was acknowledged, but not given a public hearing. The physical cause of death was clear, but there were complications regarding it. The inquest was adjourned.

The dead girl's letter did, however, indicate a certain measure of guilt, though it was not a confession of deliberate murder. For the police it was enough to transfer the continuing investigation to Detective Superintendent Farrer. With his assistant, Detective Sergeant Goff, he went over the collected evidence with particular stress upon all that connected Sister Hallet with the night nurse during the two periods of the latter's duty when she was in charge of the dead woman.

"Hallet realised Wilson's addiction and told her so," Superintendent Farrer said. "You've read the words she used as reported by the patient, Miss Parker?"

"Yes, sir."

"Then there was Nurse Biggs's evidence. From two beds away she heard Hallet, conscious again after her operation, say 'Up to your tricks again?' Another reference to Wilson's addiction, I suppose?"

"It was Wilson she said that to?"

"The night nurses were doing their rounds just before midnight, giving sleeping pills and injections and so on, as ordered."

"Another provocation, if Wilson had some idea of giving Hallet the chop."

"Using all three doses provided for the operation cases, Graham having refused his, Parker getting a dud."

"I see, sir. But would Wilson have done herself out of the dope she might have used?"

"She was getting supplies from Mrs. Camplin. Incidentally there's no trace of Camplin; the house in Barnet where the second taxi took her was empty two days later. She's probably out of the country by now. It was three days before ports and airports were told to look out for a dame with scars on her face, or painted over scars or an eastern head covering."

"But she was identified as a suspected drug smuggler and pusher wasn't she, sir?"

"Indeed, yes. Thanks to those before and after pictures

taken by the registrar. Bit of luck, that. The cosmetic surgeon, Mr. Turner, only had very technical photos, just to record exactly what he'd done to the face. Not much help with identification. Our records are several years old: she seems to have slipped up only once or perhaps did not dare to come here again."

"A bit rash, wasn't it, to get her face changed here?"

"You can say that again. But Mr. Turner has a world-wide reputation for making new faces after accidents, burns and that."

The two men were silent for a time, turning over their notes and reports, considering.

Then Detective Superintendent Farrer said, "Unless Nurse Wilson was in a desperately confused state I don't believe she would have given the injections in the way they must have been given. It was clearly a deliberate action."

"But she wasn't all that confused," Sergeant Goff added. "Because in Nurse Biggs's report she says after she finished her part of the round she found Nurse Wilson in the ward kitchen getting their midnight meal ready."

"Also the Ward Sister won't have it that Wilson was capable of pushing a dirty injection into Miss Parker's arm. What with, anyway?"

"Why not her own syringe, as she was a junky?" suggested Goff, brightly.

"That's an idea. But did she have a syringe of her own? You'd better check with Inspector Holmes and the mortuary."

"Yes, sir."

It was old Mrs. Mitchell, talking to Patty Shaw, who developed the growing certainty in Hunter Ward that the late Miss Hallet had been murdered. Her death, as even Sister Baker now agreed, must have been brought about deliberately. Mrs. Mitchell suggested there was a wide variety of motive, of malice aforethought, too, in the ward, one way and another.

As she said to Nurse Shaw, "We all know that poor Moll Wilson had a grudge against Sister Hallet. That self-righteous attitude and sharp tongue were very hurtful. I know I felt the snub she gave me more than anything I've suffered for years. With Moll it was dangerous as well."

"To Moll, you mean? She'd have been sacked pretty soon if she'd lived. I think that's why she killed herself."

"Perhaps. But what I mean is there were others with a grievance against Miss Hallet. Mine was a little one, but there was the scandal over Dr. Thompson, a wicked, cruel, libel, that. He was dreadfully upset."

"Until he got engaged to Dr. Fisher," Patty put in quickly.

"Quite so. Perhaps I ought not to have referred to it."

"Perhaps not. I wasn't going to mention it to the Law myself until I knew Miss Adams had overheard it, too."

"Anyway, I do know Mrs. Armstrong was snubbed by Sister Hallet. She told me herself that Sister Hallet wouldn't let her sweep her cubicle and called her a black bitch."

Patty laughed, which shocked Mrs. Mitchell.

"Sorry," the girl said, "but I just don't see our dear old black mammy sticking needles into Hallet with malice aforethought."

"You are much too free with your speech, my dear," said Mrs. Mitchell stiffly. "I think you should be more careful. This is not a laughing matter."

11

Though Guy made no passes and his conversation remained strictly impersonal, even boring, Patty thought, she continued to accept his now weekly invitations to dine. She enjoyed his company, while regretting his motive. For he made it very plain that the mystery surrounding the recent events in Hunter Ward still obsessed him and he found relief from its interference with his work only in discussing it with her.

Not that she could offer any direct help. How could she? The two inquests stood adjourned. Though Detective Inspector Holmes had been moved from the case Detective Superintendent Farrer had made no progress at all, or none that he had disclosed. In fact he very seldom appeared in the ward.

"You haven't actually seen him since he took over?" Guy asked, as they proceeded with their modest but well cooked meal at Guy's favourite small local restaurant, The Patio.

"Not since the first day he came. That was simply a re-cap by all of us in the ward. Before nearly everybody left, I mean."

"That reminds me. I haven't been up to see Daphne Parker for two days."

"She survives," Patty told him, with a straight look that made him redden.

"Sorry."

She laid down her knife and fork, putting them side by side English fashion, not aping the continental way with which some of the other diners, proud of recent holidays abroad, tried to impress the foreign waiter.

"It's just that we always talk shop exclusively," she complained. "I've told you nothing new has happened in the ward, so can't we talk about something else."

"Such as?"

"Well..." She fought desperately to find an outside subject, but failed. Obviously nothing but the Case held any interest for him. After her impulsive bit of sarcasm he wouldn't want to take her out again, she decided, miserable, but still defiant.

"Well," she began again, "I've just come to the end of my day stint in Hunter. I'm due for three months night duty."

He looked at her without any change of expression. Now really annoyed, she said, "Actually in Hunter."

That did shake him. "You can't!" he said, his voice rising. "You bloody well mustn't!"

"Why on earth not? Moll Wilson is dead, Sister Hallet's dead, Daphne's arm is practically healed, Mr. Campbell saw her today and he asked where you were, incidentally."

"That's a lie! He told me not to bother to come up with him. We'd just finished a list in the theatre. He let me do a strangulated hernia, resection of gut, well most of it."

"Most of the op., or most of the gut?" Patty asked, feeling herself in the ascendant.

"Op., you clot!"

They both laughed suddenly. Guy reached for her hand across the table.

"I don't want you to ask for night duty in Hunter," he said, in a new voice, low and decidedly tender, Patty thought. She felt her eyes prick with unexpected tears.

"But why?"

"I have a feeling it isn't all over yet up there. I know Moll turned out to be a junky. But I don't think she killed Hallet by accident *or* on purpose. But I do think the old girl was murdered and while the Law is still active *someone* must be getting frightened and that makes people turn very nasty, especially if they were nasty before."

"There'll still be Nurse Biggs," Patty said. "She's a real tower of strength, Sister always says."

"What does anyone really know about Nurse Biggs?" Guy asked, thoughtfully.

At St. Edmunds Nurse Biggs welcomed Patty's appointment to night duty in Hunter. The work was much lighter now and though she had not been asked to leave this emergency job, she knew it would not last much longer and then she might be assigned by her agency to some new crisis, with all that it might bring in overwork and anxiety. There were many more hospitals where the lay staff were reaching for naked power over the doctors, the patients forgotten. So the presence of Patty Shaw, with her cheerful efficiency excusing her rather touching lack of experience, came as a great relief to the older woman.

Of course, there was scarcely enough work in Hunter Ward now for two nurses. Miss Lewis, the Matron, or Senior Nursing Officer, as Bureaucracy, with its usual vice for inventing long-winded, vague, titles now called her, had already said so to her juniors, the No. 9 and No. 8 grade Nursing Officers, formerly Deputy Matrons. But the police had asked for no change to be made in the usual personnel, except to replace the dead nurse. Patty had not been chosen for ability, but because she seemed keen to go on night duty when most of the suitable candidates for the job would probably refuse from motives of conventional terror. Besides, Detective Superintendent Farrer had approved strongly. Nurse Shaw had shown great common sense and clear thinking in her first interview with him. He had every confidence in her behaviour if some new evidence came to light, he told Miss Lewis.

"New evidence?" she was shocked. "Surely you don't expect any further trouble in that ward?"

"The case is not closed," the Superintendent told her. "Nurse Wilson's death prevented us getting a clear picture of how Sister Hallet came to die of an overdose of narcotic drug. There could be some fresh development.

"God forbid!" Miss Lewis exclaimed. "I suppose you have warned the governors of the way you are risking my nurses' peace of mind, if not their well-being. Or even their *lives*!" she finished, having worked herself up to this horrifying climax.

Farrer soothed her with a few straight words.

"All the evidence we have so far," he said, "suggests that Nurse Wilson gave the overdose in a panic because Miss Hallet had guessed her addiction and had accused her of it. But we have not proved this, so we cannot yet have the two inquests resumed and finished. I have said this in strict confidence, of course."

He said no more, knowing that the S.N.O. would

inevitably spread his words to selected highly placed colleagues, from whom they would spread slowly, strictly in confidence, to the rest of the nursing staff and beyond. But not, probably, to the newsmen, or not effectively, since Wilson's case was still *sub judice.*

Nurse Biggs retailed it to Patty on the third day of their first week together, as they sat, eating a well-produced, savoury, shepherd's pie with mushrooms, for their midnight dinner.

"I must say these outside caterers know their stuff," Nurse Biggs said. "No luxury, like in some of the private nursing homes I've been in, but good value, don't you agree?"

"Yes," said Patty, who had been brought up on a farm, where the food was real and local, if monotonous. "Don't you want to go back to the luxury? I know I would."

She sighed, thinking of Guy and his lovely little restaurant dinners and his latest hint that he cared at least for her safety. She began to tell Nurse Biggs about this — well, friendship. You couldn't call it 'affair'. He did seem to fancy her a bit, though. Perhaps it was still only his interest in the Wilson-Hallet case.

It was then that Nurse Biggs passed on the superintendent's conclusions.

"But Guy thinks it's quite certain Moll did old Hallet on purpose," Patty exclaimed.

"Does he, indeed? I bet he can't prove it any more than Mr. Farrer can."

"We'll just have to keep our eyes and ears open, won't we? Guy said to tell him if I noticed anything."

"Better tell the police, my dear. It's their pigeon, not ours. Nor Mr. Harper's."

Patty had to agree, but she felt a renewed sense of

urgency in the matter. Before long, now, Hunter Ward would be empty, except for Mr. Gates, who was not much better and poor Lionel, who would never be any better.

Mrs. Mitchell, too, was staying on, refusing to go, relying on Dr. Thompson, as she told Patty on her fourth night on duty.

"Dr. Thompson never suggests I leave until I feel quite strong enough again to look after my little home," she said to Patty, when the latter brought her the usual mild sleeping pill and her nine o'clock cup of hot drinking chocolate. "Thank you, dear. I couldn't do without these. When I feel too tired at home to warm the milk I never get a proper night's sleep. Tossing and turning into the small hours. I'm just not *ready* to leave yet. All the upset in the hospital this year, so unlike the usual peace and comfort. And not over yet, is it. Those devils of porters —"

"It's all of them, I'm afraid," Patty interrupted. "All the lay staff, I mean. A sort of misplaced envy of the consultants in a way, I think. Not only the pay, the private practice, the independence that goes with managing your own life your own way." She blushed for she was quoting Guy now, almost word for word.

"Power! Independence!" snorted Mrs. Mitchell. "Ridiculous nonsense! You don't know what you're saying. You upset me!"

"I'm sorry, Mrs. Mitchell," Patty was alarmed. "I think we've all been a bit upset. Drink up, now, and here's your pill. Now the pillows. There now, don't worry. Dr. Thompson will be up in the morning."

Mrs. Mitchell did as she was told and lay back on her pillows and shut her eyes and said good night, but when Patty had shut her door she got up and opened it again and listened. Mr. Gates was talking to Nurse Shaw but in too low a voice for her to hear, which annoyed her. Gates knew something. She too knew something, that dear fat Mrs. Armstrong had told her. She wanted to know more. She had no intention of leaving the hospital until her nagging curiosity was satisfied. Presently, feeling dizzy as her pill began to work, she went back to bed and to sleep.

Fred Gates greatly approved of Patty's transfer to night duty. While he had been just as aware of Moll Wilson's addiction as Mr. Graham, he did not share that experienced sailor's calm dealing with it in relation to himself. He allowed Nurse Wilson to do for him all she was directed and had been trained to do, while he quaked with inward, stiffly controlled nervousness. On the other hand Nurse Biggs, very efficient, with her posh accent, her easy assumption of authority, made him feel awkward. Besides, she was agency, therefore on the make in a freelance capitalist manner, not, like his union, by the decision of the block vote. Nurse Shaw was a ray of sunshine compared with those two. He could chat with her about his illness, when he wasn't in a fit of coughing and breathless.

"You do talk, Mr. Gates," Patty said, laughing as she rolled him gently about, remaking his bed before settling him for the night. She pulled out a hidden packet of cigarettes from the open end of a pillowcase. "Naughty, naughty! Dr. Thompson thinks you've given them up."

He grabbed at them and pushed them back.

"Reduce them. That's all I promised. So I 'ave an all, but it's murder, I can tell you."

The word, though used in a familiar phrase, struck deep into both their minds. They stared at one another then Gates said, "I know why Farrer's been up here asking questions. Detective Superintendent. You don't get that rank on a job unless they think there's been a killing, — deliberate, I mean."

"I know," Patty said. "They go over it again and again. Every least thing that happened in the ward that night. Only there wasn't much, was there?"

"Not after midnight, there wasn't. Until that silly cow next to me here started yelling her head off in the early hours."

"The ward wasn't quiet at all before midnight, was it?"

"No, you're damn right, it wasn't. That Sister Hallet coming round from her anaesthetic and calling out in that voice of hers. Well, not exactly calling, like 'er usual, but audible enough. Me and Nurse Biggs both 'eard 'er, see. 'Up to your old tricks?' she says, asking the question, sarky like."

"And poor Moll Wilson trying to answer back, only able to whisper."

"Only it *wasn't Nurse Wilson, that wasn't.*"

Patty froze. Only for a second, but it broke the flow of reminiscence in Mr. Gates.

"Who then?" she asked quickly, breathless.

It was lost, her moment of discovery. Mr. Gates, too, was breathless, speechless. She propped him up, holding him forward. When he had recovered she eased him back, gave him his two pills with a glass of water, finally tucked him in.

"Who?" she asked gently, prepared to say good night and leave him.

"Never you mind," he grunted, and shut his eyes.

As she organised the midnight meal Patty tried to decide if she ought to tell her colleague about Mr.

Gates's statement or keep it to herself until she could pass it on to Guy. When they were halfway through the meal, however, her natural excitement got the better of discretion and she blurted out what she had heard.

To her astonishment Nurse Biggs merely looked thoughtful and took another mouthful of chicken. Then she said, "Of course I've wondered. I heard Sister Hallet's remark quite distinctly. The answer was almost a whisper. But as Nurse Wilson was the only other person in the ward except for the patients I naturally concluded it was she. Especially as I knew she had been giving herself a fix of some sort and wouldn't be quite normal. Hallet's remark fitted that, too, of course."

"Yes," Patty hesitated before she went on. "So there must have been someone else in the ward pretending to be a nurse, I suppose."

"Now that everyone seems to think Miss Hallet was killed deliberately, if Gates is speaking the truth and thinks he knows who that was, he ought to tell Superintendent Farrer or the sergeant."

"Ought we — I mean you, — to report what Gates said to me?"

"You can if you like. I won't. He didn't say it to me and I have no intention of upsetting him by referring to it."

Patty agreed that Gates must not be upset again, but she managed to get a note to Guy of possible new light on their problem. He was delighted to have another opportunity of seeing her at once for a quick breakfast-like meal before she went off duty. One remark in Nurse Biggs's careful, reported comment on the fresh information struck Guy as significant.

"Of course," he exclaimed, repeating what Nurse Biggs had said, as repported by Patty. " 'Nurse Wilson was the only other person in the ward except for the patients.' Exactly. The patients. So —"

"Oh my God!" Patty was shocked. "One of them, relatively mobile, who hated Sister Hallet?"

"Without any real medical knowledge, but knowing enough of the routine to give those three doses to her and a faked one, contaminated, to poor old Daphne."

"So who could fill the bill?"

"Can't think. Oh, Lord, look at the time! I'm due in the theatre!"

"Poor you! Go on thinking of the possibilities, Guy. I will, too. I'm off to bed."

"Lucky darling. Wish it was me, too."

She left him quickly at the door of the Nurses Home. He did not try to stop her, as he usually did now, to kiss her briefly. But she did not mind; he had called her his lucky darling; he had wished for bed, too. That was progress — of a sort. Nothing in it, of course. He meant his own bed, not hers. Stupid cat!

The next day Mrs. Mitchell was given a letter from the governors of the hospital. It asked her in dignified and pompous words that did not hide their distracted anxiety, for her co-operation in consenting to leave Hunter Ward in two days' time. Dr. Thompson was willing to discharge her, but only with her full consent. The present emergency — etc. — etc.

Weak-kneed, wobbling jellies, Mrs. Mitchell told herself. Of course I'm not ready to leave yet. It would be the greatest mistake.

She sent a very short answer to the governors, declining to oblige them.

12

Sister Baker, having lost Patty for day duty in Hunter Ward, found her replacement more trouble than she was worth. The new probationer, very young, Far Eastern, with an enchanting little round face, smooth deep-cream skin, shining blue-black hair and very poor English, preserved a commendable patience under rebuke, but did not seem able to learn.

"I could manage perfectly well with Nurse Street alone," Sister complained to Miss Lewis. "After all we have only four patients left in Hunter and two of them are men. Well, Lionel is fourteen and more sensible than most men, poor kid."

"But the other two are female. Nurse Street cannot be expected to do everything for them."

"They need very little. Miss Parker's arm is quite healed; she'll be away any time now. The strikers are getting round the governors to move Mrs. Mitchell."

"And look like succeeding," said Miss Lewis sourly. "All the same, Sister Baker, you must keep Nurse Chu for a while yet. She ought to be able to improve her English in the quiet of Hunter and with you to train her."

"She doesn't train," Sister argued. "She just stares at you, perfectly polite, no expression in those half-covered black eyes and you don't know if she's taken in a single word. To judge by her actions, not a single word. And no answer except 'Velly well, miss'. I'd much rather get on with Tim Street by himself."

"How does he get on with Nurse Chu?" asked Miss Lewis, on a sudden impulse.

"Far too well. I've not actually... But I wouldn't be surprised —"

"Give him a word of warning then. Or I might replace him with another little Nurse Chu."

"God forbid!" cried Sister Baker.

But Miss Lewis only laughed.

The nursing problem in Hunter did soon appear to be drawing nearer to a final crisis, after which the ward might be expected to begin to admit a fresh series of strictly amenity patients. For Daphne Parker had another nightmare and this time decided to go home at once.

It happened two days after Patty had discussed the hysteric's former seizure with Mr. Gates, or rather the events of the night when that outburst had taken place.

Miss Parker had not woken up screaming a second time. Neither Patty nor Nurse Biggs had heard a noise of any kind from her cubicle all night. But when Patty had gone there in the early morning she had found Daphne lying flat on her back, white-faced, breathing hard, shrunk so deep in the bed that only her face was visible above the sheet she was clearly clutching round her under the blankets.

"*Now* what's the trouble?" Patty said cheerfully, thinking, 'Oh the god-awful bore! What's eating her now?'

"Oh, it's you," Miss Parker said, emerging a little from her cocoon, but speaking in a very shaky voice. "You won't believe me, you're such an extrovert. But I swear it. I saw her again, or I dreamed I saw her, I don't know which, but I've been dreading every footstep since I really woke up. Terrified it was her."

"Who, for pity's sake?" Patty cried. "What on earth d'you mean?"

"That awful old witch! The one who gave me the abscess in my arm! She was here again. Or I must have dreamed it!"

"Dreamed it," said Patty firmly. "I'll get you a cup of tea. The kettle's just on the boil."

Miss Parker made no further complaint but when the night nurses had gone off duty and Sister Baker came on, Daphne demanded to see Dr. Thompson as soon as possible and also Mr. Campbell, because she was not going to spend another night in this murdering, haunted place.

Ian Campbell sent a message from the operating theatre that since Miss Parker's appendicectomy had been entirely satisfactory and the abscess in her arm had healed without leaving more than a minimal scar and no functional defect in the muscle involved, there was no reason why she should not go home, provided the medical side of her case met with similar approval.

David Thompson was perfectly willing to provide a companion note of approval, but Joan, originally in charge of the case in the public ward, persuaded him to see the girl in order to discharge her in person.

"It's all very well for Ian," she explained. "We must allow his operation did indeed solve the main problem."

"Which was her continual tummy pain that her G.P. thought purely neurotic."

"Exactly. A truly, if mildly, infected appendix. But the girl's a neurotic, an hysteric, if you like. If we don't butter her up, make nothing of this new vision of hers, she'll discharge herself and accuse us of neglect and I don't know what-all. With the newspack howling outside the hospital all day, it might blow up dangerously."

"How right you are, my darling. Come on, let's climb to Hunter Ward now."

They did so; they comforted and explained matters to Miss Parker at great length and on Joan's part with real sympathy. David, whose chief interest lay in what he persisted in calling 'real disease' could not but feel a basic indifference over the psychiatrist's 'meanderings in the pit', by which he meant the usually grimy and always unsavoury and devious subconscious mind.

Not that the end results on each side of medicine differed very greatly. In his 'real disease' diagnoses, backed as they were by more and more clever technology, became more and more exact, but treatment and cure made only marginal advance. As Joan forced him to agree on the many occasions when they discussed the matter.

This morning, leaving Bed 3, they were in complete accord. Only to be met, in Sister Baker's room, by Detective Superintendent Farrer, who was far from pleased to hear their verdict.

"Discharge Miss Parker?" he complained. "After what she says she saw last night?"

"So you've been told that, have you?" Dr. Thompson said, grim-faced.

"She's very unreliable," Joan put in. "She says herself it might have been a dream. She is inclined to dramatise everything that happens to her."

"Including an abscess in her arm that may have been the work of a criminal lunatic?" asked Farrer.

There was silence. They all knew the present state of the police investigation. The search was going forward to discover someone other than Nurse Wilson, someone with a more clear, more long cherished grudge against Sister Hallet, who could have been in the ward that night to administer the fatal dose. Of all the possible suspects most of those patients capable of such a deed had left. Only old Mrs. Mitchell remained. And of useful witnesses, only Miss Parker and Mr. Gates. And now the girl was going, so only the man was left.

Sister said, "Why do you object to Miss Parker going home? She won't be going away from there. You can interview her now, if she'll let you."

The doctors said nothing. If the night nurses had made no report, except in respect of Daphne Parker; if they had not seen or heard any person other than one another, in the ward that night, was it likely there really had been someone, and that person a re-appearance of the girl's previous nightmare attacker?

But the Superintendent was thorough and persistent. He was not inclined to write off Miss Parker's vision as imaginary. For Mrs. Mitchell, whom he had seen earlier that morning, had been sure she had heard footsteps, shuffling footsteps, in the region of the bathroom and lavatory at the end of the ward that very night. She explained that now she was feeling better she did not call for a bedpan at night, but saved the nurses by going along by herself and she had heard...

Farrer went along there too and made one discovery that might be significant, he thought. The fire-escape exit door was unlocked. He knew this was done originally to help the outside caterer. But after pickets had been stationed at the foot of the escape another method of entry for the food had been found. He would have to discuss this with the night nurses again.

So he held his interview with Miss Parker, who was quite ready to describe her nocturnal experiences at great length and with very little coherence. However, her description of the so-called visitor was plain enough for him to note it down. It also confirmed his view, already formed, that the present state of confusion in the hospital due to the breakdown in services by the lay staff, meant that the place was open to invasion, undetected, by any person of determination, anyone who, if accosted, could pretend to offer help in the emergency. Anyone, too, engaged to help, and there had been several, working in various capacities, known and listed. There could be others, unknown. It was up to him to vet the listed ones and discover the rest. In his next discussion with Sergeant Goff he assigned most of this work to the sergeant, keeping one main inquiry to himself.

To the surprise of the nurses and doctors looking after Hunter Ward Mrs. Mitchell, who had stood out for her rights and privileges as a paying patient, gave notice of her intention to leave, only one day after Daphne Parker went home.

True, there had been another ultimatum from Joe Wells. In a note expressing all of the original complaint in the longest possible words, with all the pompous arrogance the head porter had developed during the struggle, there was for the first time a hint of weariness. Not weakness, not yet any doubt of the righteousness of their cause, the absolute necessity to bring anxiety and suffering to sick individuals in the cause of social justice.

Oh no. But a kind of desperation that one, old, obstinate woman could continue to deny them the victory they were so near to claiming.

And at last Mrs. Mitchell was leaving. In fact, to deny Joe Wells an open triumph, she left by car from the foot of the fire-escape, like the mayor, the picket there having been removed when the escape was no longer used by the caterer. She left for home with her companion-housekeeper, who had also been enjoying rest and recuperation during Mrs. Mitchell's stay in hospital.

When safely in her own house Mrs. Mitchell got in touch with Detective Superintendent Farrer. She wanted to give him some information that might help him.

"Why did you not tell me this at the hospital?" he asked her when he answered the call to her home.

"I was afraid to. Miss Parker was not imagining a stranger in the night. I both heard and saw her, more than once."

"You *saw* her? You saw a woman?"

"Only her back. But quite recognisable."

Farrer was outraged.

"And kept this to yourself until now?"

"I was afraid, I tell you. She must be getting desperate. With me and Mr. Gates knowing."

"*Gates*? He swears he knows nothing."

"He told Nurse Shaw. I heard him. He told her that it definitely wasn't Nurse Wilson who gave Sister Hallet her overdose. He said he knew who it was whispering to Hallet and then to Miss Parker. So when I caught sight of her, creeping about in the corridor, listening outside the curtains —"

"Who?" Farrer exploded.

"That funny little V.A.D., of course. Middle-aged,

dumpy, watery eyes, big rough hands. Terribly willing, Sister always says. I think the name was Norris, but you can easily find out."

"Thank you," the Superintendent said and rose to go.

Norris. Miss M. Norris. Mary. Of course he knew. A V.A.D. in the war when she was an adolescent girl. One of two sisters. Always lived at home. Nursed her ageing parents in their last years. Taken on for duty in Hunter Ward and in Ward VI during the emergency and when most of the patients there were discharged, in the women's general medical ward until two days ago. Now back at home.

All this from Sergeant Goff's notes. He would have to check personally, Farrer decided. Mrs. Mitchell was a bit too positive. Perhaps she *was* afraid of the V.A.D. But she did not give him the feeling that she scared easily. Perhaps the fear was of him and for herself, he wondered.

No, that was fanciful. But this whole problem was so essentially low-key, he thought angrily. A very quiet, sneaking vicious murder, in a dangerous, non-violent, but almost criminal general situation where the love of power over-ruled all former tradition of service, all former dedication to the treatment of sick persons. Detective Superintendent Farrer, on his way to St. Edmunds Hospital again to confront Mr. Gates with what Mrs. Mitchell had said, thought he would far rather go to one of the pubs where his regular informers kept him up to date with prospective breakings and raids and snatches, with the threat of rough violence and rapid counter-action, than continue to investigate in that distorted hospital atmosphere.

But he continued on his way to St. Edmunds and found all the lifts in working order with Armstrong, his white teeth gleaming in a wide grin on his dark face, pressing the knob for the fourth floor and announcing their arrival, "Hunter Ward, sah," as he opened the lift gate.

The lay staff's ban was lifted: all services were back to normal.

But Fred Gates was worse. When Farrer found Sister Baker with his request to see the union official she refused him point blank.

"Impossible!" she said firmly. "He's had difficulty with his breathing again ever since Mrs. Mitchell went to say goodbye to him yesterday morning. I don't know if she said anything to upset him; she was a bit of an old busybody, you know. Or perhaps you don't. But there it is. I've got him in an oxygen tent. Dr. Thompson has given orders he is not to speak to anyone except us and he's not to write any more letters."

"Letters?" Farrer was astonished. "You don't mean to tell me he's been conducting his union business from here in spite of his illness?"

"I do not. But Mrs. Gates was up seeing him yesterday afternoon and she came to me asking for note paper as he wanted to write a letter, which he says he did and gave it to her to post."

"Then you don't know who it was addressed to?"

"I do not. Only that Mrs. Gates took it away and she agreed with me he must not write another until he is over this new attack."

In the corridor, after he left Sister Baker, the Superintendent met Nurse Street.

"Fresh trouble for Mr. Gates, I'm told," he said with some hope of further detail.

"Yah. Poor bastard's really bad today," Tim answered cheerfully. "Oxygen an' all. Looks bloody worried.

Dr. Joan says he's not been obeying orders to stop smoking. That makes him mad, but it's true."

"He won't be able to smoke in an oxygen tent, will he?"

"Too right, he won't. But it isn't only that. There's things on his mind."

"Know any of them?"

Tim stared suspiciously, then turned away, muttering under his breath, "Think I'd spill a patient's confidences to a pi — to a copper?"

Farrer turned away. Stupid young puppy, he thought. Fashionable nonsense. Perhaps he had seen the address on the envelope of Gates's letter. Or Mrs. Gates might have shown it to him. Non-co-operative. Far too much of it.

Just outside the ward he came across Nurse Chu going in. She gave him an enchanting smile and said. "Lifts all coming now, sir," and pointed the way with a small, straight, cream-yellow finger.

He hesitated and Nurse Chu stood still, waiting, polite, wary.

"You have met the patient, Mr. Fred Gates?" he asked at last.

She shook her head.

"I no speak velly much English," she said softly, still waiting, still polite, now quite unapproachable.

"Never mind," he said and made for the lifts with hand upraised to press the button for descent.

On his desk when he got back to his office he found the letter from Fred Gates. It had been handed in by his wife about an hour before. It was addressed to him personally. It presented information that did not startle him but confirmed an idea that he felt was rapidly becoming a certainty.

13

WITH HUNTER WARD no longer blacked, St. Edmunds Hospital was relieved of more than half the number of visiting journalists. They had swarmed into the main hall every morning, to bait the chief porter, or offer him sympathy and support, according to the political views of the papers they served. One or two freelance men still came, because of the interest attaching to Sister Hallet's death; the now rumoured manslaughter, if not murder. But though these few self-appointed sleuths dug out evidence of continued police activity, they did not manage to speak either to Detective Superintendent Farrer or his assistant, Detective Sergeant Goff. The two detectives did visit the hospital fairly often, but in such a rabbit warren of a place it was impossible to track them down.

Moreover the journalists found that Joe Wells, diminished after victory, most unfairly, he considered, was not willing to help them. He had fallen from the temporary dizzy pinnacle of power to his old status at the front entrance of the hospital. Power of a sort, of course. He could dispose of ordinary visitors, inquiries, patients, as they entered. But a stern word from the chairman of the governors about taking care not to exceed his duty unless he preferred redundancy, had brought his feet slapping down to earth quite painfully. In self-defence, ego-deflated defence, he treated all journalists now with stern hauteur, even a lecture on the subject of the basic right of hospitals, doctors and lay staff alike, to protect the privacy and well-being of the victims of disease. Ribald and scurrilous replies from thwarted amateur sleuths did not disturb him.

"And you can take the grin off your monkey face, Armstrong," he shouted at the lift porter. "Bloody snoopers! Public interest, my arse! Get on up with those supplies for Hunter Ward!"

"Yes, Mr. Wells," Armstrong replied meekly, reserving his derision and his resentment for the sympathetic Mrs. Armstrong at home.

In the kitchens Eric Hill wrote out fresh menu lists for Hunter Ward. The two remaining patients there were on restricted diets, but seemed to be staying in hospital for a further protracted, if indefinite period. Still, this meant that he was providing only two sets of meals and that affected his salary, though not very seriously.

He spoke to the Hospital Secretary, who took him to see Dr. Thompson.

"Yes," the latter said. "I agree we have waiting lists and these are empty beds, four for private patients and six for amenity cases. But the governors suggest we do not admit private cases and the consultants have agreed to that. In fact, most of us have arranged to place them in other hospitals or private nursing homes. A few foreigners have cancelled altogether and will go to other countries. It won't be long before the consultants will follow them," he added ominously.

"But the amenity beds?"

"Well, we've been asked to fill them from the general wards. I don't know about my colleagues, but my own patients have said 'No, thank you'. Some of them don't want to pay two or three quid a week for the privacy. They prefer community life, non-stop radio and television, endless gossip. The only ones who would like the amenity, nervous characters mostly, are scared of Hunter as the 'murder ward'. Much too scared to want to move up there."

"Does that apply to the men as well?"

"I'm talking of both sexes. The men are more scared than the women, it seems. More naturally superstitious, I suppose."

"I thought it was the other way round."

"Don't you believe it."

So the Secretary and Mr. Hill went away to their respective departments and Dr. Thompson went up to Hunter Ward where he found Detective Superintendent Farrer talking to Sister Baker. He told them about the caterer's complaint.

Sister was anxious to see the ward filled again, but Farrer was not.

"Not until we've cleared up the Hallet case," he argued. "Unless, of course, you need the beds filled, doctor."

"Why not? I mean why do you want the beds empty?"

"I can't tell you at the moment. But our inquiries look like being, well, productive, within the next day or two and —"

"Can't you explain without all that guff? Are you telling me you have found the culprit who knocked off Sister Hallet? If so, why not say so?"

"I don't think you'd really like me to do that, sir."

"I certainly *would*! We're not children, Sister and I."

"No, sir. But you have a couple of sick patients here just now and I consider it my duty to protect them to the best of my ability."

"*You* would like to protect them? *Your* duty? What the hell does that mean? What about *my duty*?"

The two men, both stiff with anger, stared at each other. Sister left them quickly. She had heard outside her room a step that she recognised.

"Oh, Dr. Fisher, Dr. Thompson and the Superintendent are going for one another about our new admissions. Do you think you —?"

But Joan had already gone, hurrying to David to save him from his touchy self. She succeeded, or enough to release the detective and persuade her David that the Law depended upon secrecy in doing their job and anyway Mr. Gates needed maximum rest and quiet, whereas an immediate influx of new patients would undoubtedly make that impossible.

"I expect you're right," he answered wearily. "At least he'll get maximum attention at night, which is when he seems to be at his worst."

This was true and turned out to be of vital importance within the next twelve hours.

Patty was sitting at the night table in the ward, writing up her notes before filing some reports on the two remaining patients, when she smelt smoke. She sniffed. Tobacco, undoubtedly. Heavy, too.

She got up and went out to Sister's room, where Nurse Biggs usually sat these days until the midnight meal. She knew that Nurse Biggs smoked; never when there was work to do, but sometimes as now, when they were particularly slack.

Nurse Biggs was reading a novel; she was not smoking. Patty explained why she was interrupting her.

"Smoke? What sort?"

"Cigarette, I suppose. I don't. Guy made me give it up. I thought —"

"You know I only use these small cheroots. But you're right! Tobacco. And... Oh, my God! Come on!"

They ran down the ward. It was filling with smoke, not only tobacco. Smouldering blanket. And in the thickening source of it the harsh, gasping, croaking voice of Mr. Gates.

His oxygen tent was hanging over the side of the bed on one side and Mr. Gates was hanging out on the other. In the middle of the bed a dull round red spot showed through the haze of a half-smoked cigarette that lay eating its way into the top blanket.

Silently they dealt with the danger and its already dangerous consequence. Nurse Biggs folded the top blanket over the start of the fire, wrapped it into a smaller package, stamped on it then rushed it to the bathroom and turned the tap on it.

Meanwhile Patty hauled Mr. Gates back into bed, propped him up, found the end of the oxygen tube that had miraculously fallen to the floor away from the source of combustion and played it near his face. At least, she thought, it is driving the smoke away and may help him till Biggs comes back, but he looks as if he's a gonner this time.

Having disposed of the fire, Nurse Biggs opened windows and doors to drive out the remains of the smoke before rapidly re-assembling Mr. Gates's oxygen tent.

By now the patient, contrary to Patty's despairing conclusion, was beginning to take deep breaths, though he was not yet capable of speech. Nurse Biggs took over from Patty while the latter called the houseman on duty. Then both nurses waited until the yawning, sleep-sodden young man arrived. He found an unexpectedly dramatic situation that woke him up at once.

"Trying to have a smoke, were you?" he said to Mr. Gates. "No, don't try to talk. Just nod if I'm right."

Fred Gates nodded miserably.

"Dropped it on the bed, did you?"

Fred shook his head.

"Wonder you didn't suffocate yourself, lighting up inside your tent. Damned dangerous. Why do it? Tobacco addict, I suppose."

Again Fred shook his head; he even tried to speak, but began to cough instead.

"Mustn't do it again," the houseman said. "Nurse'll give you something — Have you got — ?" he went on, speaking to Patty as she followed him out of the cubicle.

"You might have killed yourself," Nurse Biggs told Mr. Gates, adding to his general sense of affront.

She had found the packet of cigarettes and the lighter in his bedside locker. She slipped them into her pocket. "You might have burned down the ward and killed us all! Lionel too!" she went on.

"Stuff it!" Mr. Gates gasped and shut his eyes.

They all had it in for him, he complained to his wife the next afternoon. No chance to explain, not that he'd be believed.

"You tell me, then," she urged. "I'll pass it on if it isn't another of your fancies."

He groaned.

"Catch you believing a word I say. I suppose you did hand in my letter?"

"Of course I did. They even give me a receipt for it."

"To cover their slackness when they don't act on information supplied."

"I wouldn't be too sure."

"Now who's being mysterious?"

"Never you mind. Dr. Thompson wants to move you to the special chest hospital. Only for this setback, he says, he'll have to keep you here another few days."

Mr. Gates accepted this and privately knew he had been at fault in trying to smoke. But he knew, too, as he had explained to Detective Superintendent Farrer in a voice too low, (but carefully recorded by the detective) for anyone else in the ward to hear, that the near disaster had not been his fault, but was a deliberate attack upon him by an enemy he recognised quite plainly.

"It's these bloody curtains," he concluded, as Farrer packed away his neat little recording apparatus. "Shut you up so you can't see who's coming or going, or waiting and listening. Dr. Thompson wants me out, so what's keeping me? Why don't you do your stuff? "

"Not enough evidence for an arrest, Mr. Gates. Nearly, but not quite."

"Waiting till they get me? That it?"

"You'll be well protected from now on. I do promise you that."

The Detective Superintendent was as good as his word. Hunter Ward, from that day, was under very careful surveillance. An extra workman in overalls appeared from the general maintenance department to make some adjustments in the bathroom, at the end of the ward and particularly near the exit door on to the fire-escape. A night watch was also provided in this region, but at ground level.

The next event, when it came, took place some

distance away, out of doors, in the near darkness of a drizzling, overcast evening.

Patty Shaw had gone up early to the ward, because she had started an unauthorised, but perfectly commendable habit of reading aloud to Lionel Cox, to fill in the otherwise empty time before he was expected to settle down for the night.

For some weeks he had grown more and more restless at this time of day. Partly this was because in general health he had improved as he still did under intensive treatment. He had reached the stage of actually needing exercise. When Sister Baker had complained to him that he must be content to go slowly, and that he must not let himself be irritable, he answered, half laughing. "That's all very well. I know I'm fitter. I know I could go for a jolly long walk — well, a walk round the grounds, if you'd only let me. If it doesn't last, as it never does, what's the odds? I've just lost out again on something I... I..."

"All right," Sister said to forestall the emotional breakdown, "Get your dressing gown on and I'll take you down to the day room in Ward VII."

"But that's the kids, isn't it?"

"Would you rather have the old gentlemen in Ward VIII?"

"Hawking and spitting and pissing their pyjamas? Sorry, Sister. I didn't mean —"

"Well, are you coming?"

"No. No, thank you. I'm all right."

But Patty, when she saw him later found him far from all right. She thought 'he sees himself fit for anything just now, and yet he knows he isn't. So he's just brooding.'

The next night she took along a copy of *Treasure Island*,

but he knew it already. She tried again with Masefield's *Jim Davis* and this time succeeded.

"At least he wasn't fretting," she explained to Night Sister, when she was making her rounds.

Nurse Biggs joined in. "It was a brilliant idea," she said. "He can imagine himself in Jim's place with the smugglers and I bet he's doing it all differently so that he wins every move that Jim loses in the book."

"You seem to know the book very well," Night Sister said rather sourly as she left them.

This had been three days after the fire in Mr. Gates's cubicle. The reading had continued and the story was so absorbing that neither Patty nor the boy had noticed how the time passed, until Mr. Gates's bedside bell rang and continued ringing.

Patty clapped the covers of the book together, tossed it to Lionel and dived between the two sets of curtains into the cubicle across the corridor.

"Where's Nurse Biggs?" Mr. Gates asked in a hoarse whisper.

"Hasn't she been in to you?"

It was at this time the agency nurse's habit to look after Mr. Gates while Patty helped Lionel.

"I wouldn't be asking you if she had," he gasped.

"Can you wait a second? I'll run and find her."

But Nurse Biggs was not in the ward. She was not in the Nurses Home. She was known to have left there to go on duty at eight o'clock. It was now a quarter past nine.

Patty rang the number Detective Superintendent Farrer had pinned up in Sister's room for help in emergencies of a non-medical kind. Then she went back to Mr. Gates.

"Mean to say she's run out on us?" he exclaimed indignantly.

"I'll never believe that," Patty answered. But her voice quavered. "I know they're all looking for her."

In the cubicle opposite Lionel sat up and listened. Though the blue light above his bed was dim he could just manage to read, so he had gone on with the story of Jim Davis after Nurse Shaw dashed away. Now something was happening in the ward. Something exciting, perhaps. He hoped so from the bottom of his heart.

In the grounds of the hospital Detective Sergeant Goff, with two night porters and Night Sister were searching for Nurse Biggs. They found her in some laurel bushes not far from the Nurses Home. She was lying on her face with a bleeding gash at the back of her head.

When they had carried her into the Home and sent for the surgical casualty officer, she began to recover consciousness. But she could only say that something had hit her from behind. She neither saw nor heard an assailant. Perhaps a tile from the roof had fallen on her.

This charitable suggestion did not appeal to Sergeant Goff. Leaving the nurse in medical care he went to report at once to Detective Superintendent Farrer.

14

NIGHT SISTER BROUGHT the news to Patty an hour later. Then she went away again, for there were two very seriously ill cases in the medical wards where her advice and direction were needed.

Patty had insisted that she could cope alone. Only two patients, for heaven's sake. But after Sister had gone Mr. Gates became insistent.

"Nurse Biggs isn't coming on duty, then? What's up with her?"

"She's had a slight accident, Sister said."

Patty left him to go across to Lionel with this news.

"Nurse Biggs? What sort of accident?"

"A fall in the grounds, coming over from the Nurses Home."

"Fall? Nurse Biggs? Broken anything?"

"I don't think so. She was unconscious when they found her. She seems to have knocked herself out."

"Not Nurse Biggs! Never!" Lionel was excited. He bounced up and down in his bed. "Bet she was coshed. Was she coshed, Nurse Shaw?"

"Hush! You'll upset Mr. Gates! Lie down now and go to sleep. It's after eleven."

Lionel obeyed, but he had no intention of going to sleep. For one thing the ward was by no means quiet. It should have been with only old Gates besides himself. But Gates was in trouble again. Oxygen and all that. Very daring, with his new strength egging him on, he crept out of bed and tiptoed to the corner of his curtain and listened.

Patty was horrified when she went back into Mr. Gates's cubicle. He was leaning back on his piled pillows, his eyes staring, his face blue, his mouth opening and shutting as he tried to force air into his lungs. The oxygen apparatus was still there beside him; it had never left his cubicle. Working fast Patty got it going again, to his almost immediate relief. But it was some time before his colour improved and he tried to signal to her that he wanted to speak.

His voice was very weak, very hoarse, but she knew that he had something sensible to say; he was not delirious.

"I seen her," he said. "Like before. Looking in at me."

"Through the curtains, you mean? In the ward?"

"Naturally. Not a blooming fly at the window, up the wall outside."

"No. No, of course. Who was it, Mr., Gates? *Both times, who was it?*"

He waited, his eyes closed. Patty began to wonder if he really had seen someone in the ward. Perhaps he was delirious, after all.

"Norris," he grated, in a renewed burst of sound that made her jump. "Millie — Maggie — Can't remember her blasted name. Her, all right, though."

Norris. Patty remembered the V.A.D. who had helped in the ward for a few days when the porters' emergency began. Yes, helped the day of Sister Hallet's operation.

"You really saw Miss Norris? Here, just now?"

He nodded.

"It was Miss Norris too, the night you set fire to your blanket with a cigarette?"

He stared at her for a second, before nodding again and then whispered, "She give me the fag."

"You had a packet in your locker."

"She must of put it there, see. She lit it up for me. Knew I'd most likely drop it. I never —"

There was a terrified look in his eyes and Patty felt it was mirrored in her own. She believed him. That funny old V.A.D. with her bustling, rather clumsy ways was and had been a malign presence, a threat, a secret attacker. Why? What possible motive could she have for troubling poor Mr. Gates? Certainly she was not a member of his union, she told herself, with a giggle she surprised in her mind. So what? And why? Why on earth?

"But Mr. Gates, why should she do these things? Why to you, for God's sake?"

"Because I knew her voice that other time. Knows I knew her."

His voice was so low now that Patty had to bend over him to hear. But the words were quite distinct and they both chilled and angered her. Why had he not told all this to the cops? Why not clear up the mystery over poor Moll Wilson and her suicide? Was that really suicide or another deliberate act by this horrible V.A.D.?

Patty alternately froze and burned as she sat beside Mr. Gates, wondering how she was to get through the night, when to leave him might bring out again the unseen visitor, not now unknown, unless his whole story was fantasy.

She thought of Guy. If, as seemed certain, Nurse

Biggs's injuries were surgical, he would have been called to the Nurses Home to deal with them. Provided he was on duty this week and therefore in residence or within easy call. She tried to remember, but could not and her diary was in the desk in the corridor. If she could leave Mr. Gates for a bit she could look up the dates. If...

A glance at her watch told her it was now just after one o'clock. A whole two hours since she had rescued Mr. Gates from his sinister visitor or his malignant vision, whichever it had been. Her mealtime had passed while she had been sitting there. She wanted her dinner — badly.

Looking about her, fully alert, determined upon action, she remembered what someone — had it been Guy? — had said about Sister Hallet's attacker. The curtains. The damned curtains, so many hiding places ready for a criminal to pass unseen from one cubicle to another, from bed to bed, from victim to victim.

Getting quietly to her feet she tiptoed to the side of the cubicle and very gently and slowly drew back the curtains from the corridor side to the wall. The rings made a slight noise but nothing happened. She repeated the action on the curtain shutting out the corridor.

As she did so she thought she heard Lionel exclaim or grunt in his sleep and paused, but the sound was not repeated. She moved to the third curtain, remembering that beyond it lay the bed where Daphne Parker had lain and suffered an outrage to her arm. She took hold of the curtain and slowly, gently, drew it from the corridor to the wall.

On Daphne's bed, crouched, squat, her fat legs dangling, sat the dowdy figure of the V.A.D., little watery eyes fixed upon her in dull rage and hate.

Patty screamed. The intruder leaped off the bed,

stumbling as her short legs reached the ground. Mr. Gates woke with a hoarse cry and thrashing arms that knocked his oxygen tent sideways: Lionel ran out from his cubicle and bounded across the corridor.

"She's got a knife!" he yelled, diving forward.

His arrival checked the woman just long enough to allow Patty to grip her wrist and twist it. She was a strong, healthy girl and fear gave her extra strength.

"Got it!" Lionel shouted as the weapon fell and he snatched it from the floor.

"The phone!" Patty gasped. "Help! Call help!"

He ran down the ward to the night table. He was out of breath; the telephone, table, the floor and the ceiling spun round before him, but he got hold of the receiver and called, "Police! Hunter Ward! Urgent! Police!" before he sank on to the nurse's chair and laid his head on the table, struggling to recover.

He was still struggling, still half-conscious, when Detective Superintendent Farrer's voice said to him, "Let go the knife, son. You won't want it now."

Lionel looked up, straightening himself as he found his vision re-focussed and his strength returning. He saw the Superintendent bending towards him and beyond them Nurse Shaw with Mr. Harper's arm round her shoulders.

He handed the knife to Farrer. He had not really looked at it before. He saw it was just an ordinary kitchen knife, not pointed, not sharp, with a bent imitation ivory handle.

He was disgusted.

"That's no good," he said. "Wouldn't hurt a fly."

"You'd be surprised," the Superintendent said gravely. "In the hands of a maniac —"

He broke off as Patty freed herself from Guy's

protecting arm and went behind the table to lift Lionel away from it.

"Back to bed, my lad," she said, shakily.

"I'm not tired. I'm O.K. Leave me alone."

"You did a first-class emergency rescue," Guy told him, taking his arm on the other side. "Anyone could flake out after that. A hot drink for this patient, nurse," he went on, winking at Patty over the boy's head. "Then sleep."

"That means *pills*," said Lionel with renewed disgust. But he got to his feet and moved slowly up the corridor, with Guy's hand under his elbow.

Patty disappeared into the ward kitchen. Farrer went to Mr. Gates's cubicle where Detective Sergeant Goff was standing beside the bed, while the union official, his eyes closed, was breathing noisily and coughing by turns, though his colour had returned to its normal yellowish brown.

Though his eyes were closed he evidently heard Farrer's footfall, for he opened them and said slowly, "Get away, did she?"

"Yes."

Sergeant Goff shuffled his feet and said, "I told him. Down the fire-escape. No need to keep it still unlocked, sir, I take it?"

"You mean you've locked it?"

"Yes, sir."

In the silence that followed, Mr. Gates said bitterly, "Joe Wells's pickets did better'n your chaps. Till the doctors went down for the grub themselves."

"My chaps, as you call them, have been combing the grounds for Nurse Biggs's assailant," Farrer told him, stung by this remark. "She wasn't found immediately. They think she'd been lying in the bushes for over two hours. Naturally we thought the attacker had left, though no one had been seen to leave. Besides —"

He broke off. He did not intend to tell this man, with his trade union prejudices, any more detail of the night's police work. He was in Mr. Gates's cubicle for quite another purpose.

So he said, moving a chair to the man's bedside, "Are you fit to answer a few questions, Mr. Gates? Say if you don't feel up to it. But we've read your letter about Miss Norris and the hospital has given me certain information about her earlier attempts to train as a nurse. But I think you could help me to fill in the picture of her home life. She lived quite near your former house, I think."

"They all did."

"All? Who, in fact?"

"Father, mother, Mary, Maisie."

"Go on."

Recovery brought no change in Nurse Biggs's account of the attack upon her. She had not seen or heard anyone as she walked through the hospital grounds on her way to Hunter Ward. All she remembered was the sudden pain of the blow, immediately followed by the sensation of falling.

She recovered very quickly. Her skull had not been broken, the gash in her scalp mended quickly. They kept her in bed for two days, by which time she had shown no signs of any cerebral damage. Then she left for her married sister's home where she usually lived between cases. After all, her job at St. Edmunds was a temporary one. Her agency was very pleased to have her back on their books. But they determined not to offer her services anywhere for at least three weeks.

"Can't risk that delayed shock we read so much about these days," they told her.

"Stuff and nonsense!" Nurse Biggs said, repeating the words to Sister Baker when she went up to Hunter Ward to say goodbye.

"Self-protection, I suppose," Sister answered. She did not approve of agencies and greedy middlemen, making a good living out of the bureaucratic incompetence of our rulers. "You'll leave your home address with the Secretary, won't you?"

"If they want it."

"Well, I think it's really the police that want it. Mr. Farrer keeps coming and going. He must be on to something. He's asked once or twice for your address and we could only give him the agency."

"That should satisfy him."

"Apparently not. So you will see the Secretary, won't you?"

Though Nurse Biggs nodded and went off up the ward to say goodbye to Lionel and Mr. Gates, Sister Baker felt uneasy. So after she had seen Nurse Biggs into the lift, she telephoned to Detective Superintendent Farrer and after that to the Secretary's office. Both answers were reassuring, but vague. Nurse Biggs was still in the hospital, talking to a friend in the Out-patient department, but they were having her paged.

Sister Baker sighed. She was depressed by the unnatural state of her ward. All those empty beds — and the waiting lists as long as ever. But, thank goodness, the emergency exit to the fire-escape was kept locked now, day and night. With the lock well oiled and easy to work and with a new, simply worded, explicit card of instruction fastened to the door just above the opening bar.

15

The Norris sisters lived in a semi-detached house called 'Belhaven' which stood with another twenty pairs, ten each side of Priory Road, about a mile from St. Edmunds Hospital and to the south of it.

The houses were of a comfortable, uninteresting, but highly respectable kind, built in the middle twenties to house an expanding commuter population. Similar buildings formed the much criticised 'ribbon' development that lined the wide new main roads from the older London suburbs. They had small garden plots behind them and had, when new, small front gardens as well. But with the growth of motor traffic since the Second World War the main roads had been widened and these little front gardens, with their roses and their gnomes had been put back to tiny strips of grass and low walls or fences.

Priory Road had not suffered in this respect. In fact it was a cul-de-sac, for the south end of it met the Green Belt and could go no further. This made it additionally 'cosy and quiet' as Miss Mary Norris explained to Detective Superintendent Farrer when he called to see her.

"We have good neighbours," Miss Norris explained. "Always do have. That makes for a cosy atmosphere, don't you agree?"

"Have you always lived here, Miss Norris?" Farrer asked, while Detective Sergeant Goff prepared to jot down notes of the conversation.

"Not quite always. I was born in Highgate, near the Heath. We came here when I was eight. These houses had not long been built. There should have been more but I think the money ran out in the slump."

"Or the Green Belt — ?"

"Nothing like that in those days, just real green fields where my father took our dog for walks."

"Instead of the present end house?"

"That was built much later, after the second war. Priory Road wasn't going anywhere by then, just closing into our little community, cosy and quiet."

"Yes," said Detective Superintendent Farrer.

The interview was going to be particularly sticky, he decided. Thick, whimsical glue was spreading over it. Any more harking back to Miss Norris's past was likely to set immovably.

He tried to struggle forward.

"So you and your family came to live here and you stayed on after the parents died?"

"I and my sister, yes. We owned the house and just enough to live on. My father had worked for a pharmaceutical firm."

Farrer knew this. A traveller in medicines to general practitioners for a well-known and highly thought of firm.

He smiled at Miss Norris.

"Which gave you your interest in medical matters, I suppose?"

Miss Norris smiled back. For the first time her face, broad and plain, with a spreading nose and small sharp dark eyes, lit up as she answered.

"Oh, yes! If I'd been clever I would have tried to become a doctor. I did go in for nursing, but —"

She had surprised herself. She had said too much, perhaps, shown an undying, unsatisfied enthusiasm she had meant to keep hidden. Her face flushed, her hands shook.

"But?" Farrer asked gently.

"I was needed more at home."

Miss Norris had recovered. She went on in her former style.

"My mother was not strong and she needed my help with Maisie."

"Your sister?"

"Yes. Three years younger than me. Delicate. Very delicate. Always getting the children's diseases, you know. Measles, whooping cough, scarlet fever. No immunity injections in those days."

She spoke about the delicate young sister quite normally, quietly, putting across, Farrer thought, a very acceptable picture of deep family devotion and service. No doubt seeing herself in the role of nurse, trained nurse, professional adviser, guiding the mother who was not strong.

The Superintendent paused. Should he go further into the question of Maisie, the delicate one, whom he knew from other sources had been born mentally subnormal and had never been to school; or should he pursue the medical thread in this tortuous labyrinth? For though Miss Norris's account of herself and her history was ordinary enough, even altogether boring, she seemed, with a subtlety that could surely not be intended, deliberate, to damp down, glue over, even perhaps misrepresent herself, her past, and also her present circumstances.

He sighed audibly, dragging his wits together. He saw Detective Sergeant Goff looking at him with open astonishment and Miss Norris staring at him with dark eyes in which now, did he imagine it, there was a distinct air of satisfaction.

"I have come to see you chiefly to check your attendance as a V.A.D. during the recent crisis at St. Edmunds Hospital," he began again, speaking briskly now and rather fast. This made Goff flip over a page of his notebook and write quickly a new heading before looking up at Miss Norris for her answer.

"I think I had better fetch my diary," she said, getting up to rummage in the top drawer of her desk that stood against the wall near to where the Sergeant was sitting.

He saw her turn over a pile of loose papers and envelopes, push aside one or two picture postcards and pull out a small red notebook with thin covers that had curled back from constant use. More of an account book than a diary, Goff thought, catching sight of some columns of figures as Miss Norris, holding it clumsily in one hand, shut the desk drawer with the other. However, once back in her former chair, she turned the pages until she came to the one she needed.

"Well?" Farrer asked.

Miss Norris gave the date of her first attendance, when she had helped out in Hunter Ward.

"That was the day Sister Hallet was admitted?" Farrer asked.

"The next day but one."

"You mean two days later?"

"Isn't that the same thing? Anyway it was the day Sister Hallet had her operation."

"Did you see her before she went down to the theatre?"

"No. But I was there when she came back."

"Did she see you?"

"She wasn't round from the anaesthetic."

"So she did not see you then, but what about later?"

"Later?" Miss Norris looked puzzled. "I was off duty later. I went home."

"And the next day?"

"She had died in the night, I was told. But after that day I worked in Ward VI, not in Hunter."

Farrer said carefully, "I have been told that you did appear in Hunter Ward from time to time after that. Sister Baker, Mrs. Mitchell, Miss Daphne Parker, all remember you. Are you saying you never saw them or spoke to them in the days following Sister Hallet's and Nurse Wilson's deaths?"

"You were asking me about my work as a V.A.D. That was all done in Ward VI. I did go up to Hunter a few times, just to see how they were getting on. I helped with cups of coffee a few times. Not to work there officially. Sister Baker understood that."

Sister Baker had been rather confused over Miss Norris, the Superintendent remembered. But the regular, loyal nursing staff were all confused at the time, deprived as they were of the regular background services upon which they depended for their freedom to attend wholly to the patients' needs. Farrer decided not to press the point.

"So you worked every day after that in Ward VI until the crisis was over?"

Looking at her diary as she turned the pages Miss Norris agreed and gave him the date of her final discharge — correctly, he thought, according to the Sister in Ward VI.

Miss Norris closed the diary and waited.

"Since then, have you on any day, morning, afternoon or evening, visited St. Edmunds Hospital, to visit a patient or for any other purpose?"

"Why no. Whatever for?"

"May I look at the diary?"

"Of course."

She handed it to him. He turned the pages, noted that it had been used from time to time for household accounts but that her recent hospital service was wholly consecutive and correctly dated.

During his inspection Miss Norris's face was unmoved, her manner as dull as ever. She took back the little book without comment.

Detective Superintendent Farrer looked at his watch. He was surprised to find how short a time he had been in this house; it felt like half a day at least. But he had no more questions to ask, nothing further to dig into, except the 'delicate' Maisie. She could keep. Her guardian, he was sure, would produce her if asked to do so and they would learn nothing from the exhibition.

Then he remembered. Getting up with some formality that signalled Detective Sergeant Goff to do likewise, he thanked Miss Norris and let her guide him to the front door. It was only when he stood on the doorstep, Goff having gone ahead to get into the driving seat of their car that he said, "Oh, by the way, I didn't check with you. In those early days of the emergency, when Hunter Ward had to be supplied by the back door, so to speak, did Sister Baker show you how to come and go by the fire-escape? The nurses were drilled in that, to get food up and so on."

"Yes, Sister Baker did show me," Miss Norris answered, as quiet and matter of fact as ever. "But I only used the fire-escape that one day when I came off duty. We V.A.D.s made a point of coming in past the porters, to show our independence."

She gave a short laugh, quite without mirth or humour, that chilled Farrer to the point of leaving her abruptly with a curt, "Goodbye, Miss Norris. Thanks for your co-operation."

Miss Norris shut the door upon him with great deliberation and a little vicious kick to make sure it was shut fast. As she turned to move back to her 'lounge' the delicate little sister, Maisie, slid rapidly down the banisters to bounce upright on her feet in the hall. She was grinning delightedly, and running up the stairs again, repeated the slide as neatly as before. She was nearly fifty and fat, but her arms were as strong as ever, Miss Norris thought, watching her.

"Stop that!" she ordered. "Come and help me in the kitchen. That policeman has wasted nearly all our morning."

Detective Superintendent Farrer was baffled. He had checked and re-checked Miss Mary Norris's record of service at the hospital: he found it matched perfectly with her description of her work. Her diary which he had seen was authentic, neatly written, correct in spelling, accurate in its dates. The writing had clearly not been written at one sitting but held the usual slight variations of weight and slope given it by some difference of pens used on different days. An elaborate forgery, concocted at the first hint of danger? No, that was far-fetched. He rejected it.

Before making another visit to 'Belhaven' the Superintendent arranged to see the only two people connected with the events in Hunter Ward who might be able to help him. These were Mrs. Mitchell and the coloured temporary cleaner, Mrs. Armstrong.

Of course, he had taken evidence from them already, together with all the other patients and helpers who had been in Hunter Ward, both private and amenity. But most of them were no longer available. The middle-eastern cosmetic patient and drug-pusher had been returned abroad through her embassy, the purser had been in time to join his ship, the secretary had found a new job in the north, the teacher a new school, the social worker, still convalescent at the seaside, had resigned her post, taking advantage of offered redundancy.

He knew all he wanted to know about Lionel Cox and about Mr. Gates. But Mrs. Mitchell had struck him as a nosey old bitch, nosey but also shrewd. As for Mrs. Armstrong — well, an alien outlook, different slant — prejudiced against him, no doubt, — but still —

Mrs. Mitchell greeted him in friendly fashion, only expressing surprise that the matter had not yet been cleared up.

"Don't tell me the inquest is still adjourned?" she said, opening her faded old eyes very wide.

"Which inquest, Mrs. Mitchell?"

"Sister Hallet, of course. Poor Nurse Wilson's was suicide, obviously. That wicked Mrs. Camplin gave her money to buy drugs and she bought them and took an overdose."

Farrer was not going to be led aside into the case of Moll Wilson. He said, "It was just a few questions I wanted to ask you, Mrs. Mitchell, about the nursing in the ward at the start of the emergency."

"Oh, yes. What more can I tell you? You have my statement."

"That is so. Now, about the extra help in the ward. You mention the V.A.D.s."

"One V.A.D."

"Miss Norris, wasn't it?"

"Yes. That was her name. But I hardly had anything to do with her. Just saw her now and then, helping with the general chores, not the actual nursing. Going in and out of the cubicles with a duster or carrying trays in the corridor."

"You saw her in the corridor?"

"Once or twice. I was able to go to the bathroom, Superintendent. I was not confined to my room."

"You say once or twice. But she was taken off Hunter Ward very soon and put on Ward VI."

"Yes. Of course. Very soon. Only Sister Hallet's death and Miss Parker's attack made the whole thing seem to last much longer, if you know what I mean."

Farrer nodded but he only said, "Can you describe Miss Norris more closely? You have put in your statement, 'short, dumpy, grey hair, about fifty or a bit more, full face, high colour'. Anything else? Expression, manner of speaking?"

"Her eyes," Mrs. Mitchell said. "Small, dark, watery-looking. Not much expression, ever. Quite ordinary speech. Didn't say much the only time she came to do my room, because Sister called her away."

A bit of luck, that, Farrer thought, as he left Mrs. Mitchell. Rewarding. Now for Mrs. Armstrong.

The Jamaican was not pleased to see him, but as he was in plain clothes she did not realise his profession until he had made his way into her small council flat. He made the same opening move as with Mrs. Mitchell. Had she anything descriptive to add to her statement about her work in Hunter Ward. The V.A.D., for instance.

"You mean that one called Norris?"

"Yes. Miss Norris. Can you tell me what she looked like?"

"Short, too fat, not young. You want her, when?"

"When you were helping in Hunter Ward." He looked at her with a friendly smile. "When your husband took you up in his lift to the top floor, hidden behind the medicine trolley."

He was quoting from her statement. She began to laugh as he hoped she might.

"Miss Norris had to walk up, I expect?"

"That one, I don' know. I see her once. In Mistress Mitchell's room. I feel — She look at me —"

"Yes?" Farrer's interest was apparent in his manner. Too much so, for Mrs. Armstrong, whose manner had been confiding, recoiled from him, muttering, "I not speak of that one. No good." She touched her forehead briefly.

"Not all there, d'you mean? Off sharp? Bonkers?"

"I not speak of that one," Mrs. Armstrong repeated strongly and to Detective Superintendent Farrer's surprise and inward alarm she whispered, "Good Lord, save me!" and crossed herself three times.

16

Two days after Detective Superintendent Farrer's visit to 'Belhaven' Miss Norris had a written communication from him. This was in the form of a letter, short but perfectly clear. The Superintendent would be obliged if Miss Norris would attend at the local police station bringing with her the birth certificates of herself and her sister, the death certificates of her parents, the deeds of possession of 'Belhaven' and her father's will, showing her right to own the house. In view of the fact that she might need a day or two to find or assemble these documents, and if necessary consult her solicitor in order to obtain copies, two dates were offered her with a request that she would let the Superintendent know which one she had chosen. There was no explanation in the letter to suggest what was the point of this demand.

Miss Norris was at first bitterly affronted and highly resentful. So much so that she immediately, upon re-reading the letter twice, to make sure she realised the full extent of the bastards' nosey interference, rang up the police station and demanded to speak to Mr. Farrer himself. Detective Sergeant Goff answered.

"It's quite simple, madam," he said politely. "Mr. Farrer understands from his interview with you the other day that you are in sole charge and responsible for your sister, who is a mentally handicapped person. He wants to make quite certain you have all the help financially and otherwise you should have."

Miss Norris exploded.

"I'm *quite* capable of looking after Maisie myself. I've done it for years. I *know* what I'm entitled to in the way of benefits and —"

"We appreciate all you've done," Sergeant Goff said and stopped, because his thoughts had switched to other, quite other, of her assumed activities and he was afraid his words might follow the thoughts to betray him.

Miss Norris too was silenced by his abruptness. Her inward fears, that had grown steadily for weeks and in wild acceleration during the last two days, now dried her mouth and rendered her speechless.

"So," Sergeant Goff resumed carefully, "can you tell me which of our suggested days will suit you best?" And not mean her doing an immediate bunk, he prayed inwardly.

"Wednesday," answered Miss Norris, equally careful and choosing a day when no callers were expected at 'Belhaven'.

"Morning or afternoon, madam?"

"Early afternoon," she answered. No need to explain that Maisie could be induced to rest after her dinner, but not before. No need, ever, until this whole business was somehow brought to an end, to make or do one single unnecessary thing.

Detective Sergeant Goff thanked her and rang off. He was not very happy with the way the call had gone, but later, when Farrer approved the day and time, he felt better about it.

At half-past two on Wednesday afternoon, therefore, Miss Mary Norris carefully and quietly locked the front door of 'Belhaven' behind her, walked briskly but without hurrying along Priory Road to the main road and turned left into it. The bus stop was about ten yards distant.

As she emerged from Priory Road, Detective Superintendent Farrer's car with Sergeant Goff driving, turned into it from the other side where they had waited until she appeared. They were not in sight when she turned her head to see if her bus was coming.

There was no answer at 'Belhaven' to repeated ringing and knocking. They gave this up very soon for they did not want to attract the attention of the neighbours. They went round to the back of the house and tried at the back door. Again, no result.

"Looks like she's out, too," Sergeant Goff suggested. "Can we break in?"

"Good Lord, no!" Farrer was shocked. "Use your loaf. We're supposed to be out on an emergency call. How long Parsons can hold Miss Norris with her documents or quite likely without them, is anyone's guess. Mary may have given the dim one something to keep her quiet and she hasn't heard the bell. She's not totally barmy, I gather. Just heavily retarded. Mental age about seven or eight."

The ground floor windows on the garden side of the semi-detached house were all shut, as were those they could see in the neighbouring half of the twin residences. Above, one of the windows seemed to be closely barred and as they compared it with those upon either side, they saw it open inwards, leaving the bars standing out clearly against a dark interior. A hand and stout, short, arm came out between the bars, the hand opened and a yale lock key fell at their feet.

"Blimey!" said Goff. "That jolly nearly got me in the eye. What the hell —"

"Our Maisie," said Farrer. "Front door by the look of it. Come on."

It did indeed open the front door and they went in quickly, closing it behind them. There was no one in the hall, the house was perfectly silent.

While Goff stood with his back to the front door in an attitude that suggested he had met the supernatural and feared it horribly, Detective Superintendent Farrer briefly opened the two downstairs rooms, then said, "Up!" and made for the stairs.

But at the foot of them he stopped. He had heard no door open or shut; he had heard no footfall. But both he and Goff heard a low chuckle of pleasure, of pride, of excitement. Then slowly, carefully, in perfect controlled balance, Miss Maisie Norris appeared sliding, as was her constant habit and achievement during the long, still enduring years of her childhood, down the banisters from the upper storey to the ground floor. She landed gently at each of two bends in the staircase and took off again without an appreciable pause. She arrived in the hall equally gently, pulled down her skirt, pulled her jumper straight and looked up at her two visitors.

"I'm Maisie Norris," she said. "You came before to see Mary."

"Yes, we did," Farrer answered. "And now we've come to see you."

"Mary's gone out." She chuckled again. "She thought she'd locked me in, but I've had the keys for a long time."

"Are they duplicate — I mean copies — of Mary's keys?"

"I suppose so," Maisie said. "I found the one for my room after the man came to change its lock. He gave Mary two keys on a string. She put one in her handbag and the other in her desk. When I went to find it I found the second front door key so I kept that as well."

"Show me the desk," Farrer said with an encouraging smile.

Maisie did so. The desk in the sitting room was not locked; nor had it been when Mary took her diary from it the other day, Farrer remembered. That had been in the top right-hand drawer beside the knee-hole space. In the left-hand top drawer that Maisie now opened, an assortment of paper slips, sealing wax, luggage labels and string also held a number of single keys, some rusty, some bent and clearly useless.

"Thank you," the Superintendent said, closing the door of the room. "It was clever of you to pick out the front door correctly from all that lot."

"I knew its shape," she said with dignity.

"Can we sit down?" he asked, seeing she was in a suitably confident mood. "I want to ask you a few questions about your recent work at St. Edmunds Hospital."

"In the porters' strike, do you mean?"

"Well, it wasn't only the porters, was it?"

"They wouldn't work the lifts. We had to use the stairs."

She pouted at the remembrance and Farrer understood why.

"The rails there are fixed in the wall, aren't they?"

Maisie's small, weak eyes opened as wide as they could. "How d'you know?"

"Because I've walked up and down them myself. How many times did you help up there in Hunter Ward?"

At first she pretended not to hear this question, then to have forgotten. At last, when Farrer persisted, she fell into dry sobbing and finally told him her sister had forbidden her to speak about her work to anyone.

"All right," Farrer told her. "Don't be upset. It doesn't matter. You helped your sister, did you? You like V.A.D. work? Did you train with your sister?"

Maisie stared at him. It was clear that she did not understand these questions at all and therefore was not upset by them. Only by her memory of Mary's order not to discuss her work with anyone.

After a few more attempts the Superintendent gave it up. He went out into the hall to call Goff down from upstairs. Maisie watched them with growing uneasiness.

"You mustn't tell Mary you came here," she repeated several times. "Mustn't know I let you in. Be very, very angry with Maisie. Bad girl. Bad — Naughty — very naughty — Bad! Bad!"

Her voice rose as her words retreated down the years to babyhood and the start of awareness, the beginnings of speech.

"Whew!" Detective Sergeant Goff said, wiping his face with his handkerchief before starting the engine of their car. "Thought she was going to throw a fit. Spitting — did you see it? Put me in a muck sweat. How those social workers —"

"They don't," said Farrer curtly. "It's another lot in homes for the really bad ones. Get going, Frank."

Back in the Superintendent's office Goff reported upon what he had discovered upstairs at 'Belhaven'. According to orders, he had avoided handling or moving anything. But he had been disturbed by what he had found, both in Maisie's room and in her sister's.

Maisie's room, the one with the barred windows, had very little furniture and what there was had been carefully chosen to withstand any destructive assault upon it. The small chest of drawers held only toys, some broken, some obviously cherished, and a few old-fashioned cloth picture books. No clothes.

The clothes of both sisters were in Mary's room, which was also furnished austerely, but more fully than the other. Maisie's room had held no mirror of any kind, but on Mary's dressing table there was a three-sided one and one door of the big Victorian wardrobe held a full-length glass mirror. Looking at himself in this Sergeant Goff could see the door of the room behind him. Hanging from hooks on the door there were three leather straps of the kind used for holding or carrying suitcases. But he did not find the cases to which they must have belonged.

The bathroom was small, with a tiny window, double glazed in opaqueglass.

"Odd," said Farrer, when Goff had finished. "But not as odd as that dog collar I noticed in the hall beside the mackintoshes, as we were leaving."

"What about it?" the Sergeant asked.

"Well, they don't have a dog, do they? There was no sign of one."

"Could have had in the past."

"Sure. But Gates didn't mention it in his letter. A fair size it was, with a whip attached to it as a lead. Sort of thing you see with alsations or boxers. Name on the collar, too. M. Norris and an address. I didn't see the address properly, but not 'Belhaven'."

"Then they must have had a dog sometime in the

past. Didn't Miss Norris say her father took the dog for walks in the fields when they moved to Priory Road?" Goff said. "People do hate throwing things away. Sentimental over animals, too. National failing."

"I can't say Miss Norris struck me as in anyway sentimental," the Superintendent said. "Anyway, where do we go from here? We know Mary Norris tried to become a nurse. She says she gave it up to look after Maisie, but from the records we know she failed her exams as a probationer and she had a very adverse report on her work from Sister Hallet. So there was a motive of sorts for doing the old woman."

"Revenge, d'you mean? Strong enough?"

"Perhaps, for someone like Miss Norris. Have you seen Inspector Holmes? He went over her documents today when she called with them to show me. She was furious in a quiet way. Refused to see Parsons. And wanted to wait till I came in from my so-called emergency. But Holmes got her to see him. She knew he'd been up in Hunter Ward after drugs, before I took over. She was reluctant even then, but she didn't raise her voice or make a scene. Just glowered at him — white face, clenched teeth, quite alarming, he says."

"Capable of anything, was she?"

"He thought so. If pushed. So do I. But we haven't a shred of proof, except that both sisters were around at St. Edmunds when the place was in chaos, so there *was* opportunity. And we have Fred Gates's letter and signed deposition. He swears he heard *Maisie's* voice answer Sister Hallet the night the old woman died and he swears it was Maisie tried to burn him and later tried to knife Nurse Shaw."

"So the treble dose for Sister Hallet would seem to have been given by one or other of the sisters."

"Or both."

"Working together, you mean? Well, that might account for the more zany actions, Miss Parker's arm, Fred Gates's oxygen tent, whereas the actual killing of Sister Hallet was done neatly and successfully. But Mary Norris has alibis."

"Too right she has. If pushed she'll put it all on Maisie, who is definitely not fit to plead."

The two men fell silent. The evidence before them was flimsy, indeed; far-fetched, any jury would decide. The inquest on Moll Wilson had found death by fully self-confessed suicide, though her letter to the coroner had not been read aloud to spare the shocked relatives. A much more likely criminal, though, than the short, thickset, respectable, middle-aged V.A.D., apart from the crude attempts to get rid of adverse witnesses.

At last Detective Superintendent Farrer stretched and yawned and pushed the case papers together.

"We need Gates again," he said. "You take him. He's gone to that high-powered chest place. Yes, that's the one. Find out about the dog and anything more he can remember about the Norris family when he and his wife lived next to them before the parents moved. To Highgate, wasn't it? I'm going to arrange a little confrontation in Hunter Ward to sort out these bloody sisters. Day after tomorrow."

"Reconstruction of the crime?" Detective Sergeant Goff asked with a broad grin. "French style? Going E.E.C. in crime, are we?"

"None of your lip, Frank Goff, or you'll find yourself back on the beat."

"Sir," said Goff, but there was laughter still in the eyes above the solemn, respectful mouth.

Miss Mary Norris arrived home at about six that evening. She had insisted upon waiting at the police station until Detective Superintendent Farrer came back from his 'emergency'. When he did so she was more than ever surprised and affronted by her very short interview with him. In fact he did not speak, after inviting her to sit down near his desk, until he had glanced briefly at her documents, placed before him by Inspector Holmes, who had been through them with her, and which he then handed back to her.

But in the interval, while she watched him closely, she noticed the cut and colour of the very ordinary dark suit he was wearing; she wrinkled her nose at the combined smells of his tobacco, the rain-damped mackintosh he had pulled off and thrown across the back of his chair before she sat down, the faint lingering scent of soap or was it what they called after-shave lotion? The room, the whole horrible police station, reeked of men and their particular smells. Never mind those two cold-eyed bitches in uniform who had escorted her to their own female toilets. She was more conscious, reminded more of the dirty old father she had hated. She shivered.

"Cold?" Mr. Farrer had asked her. "Would you like a cup of tea?" And the Sergeant who was always with him half rose.

"*No!*" she had cried. "I want to go home, if you've *quite* finished! You and your phoney questions!"

"Not *quite* finished," Mr. Farrer had answered. "But go home, by all means. And thank you for your co-operation."

So now she was back, after all that time, and she really could do with a a cuppa. But the moment she opened the door of 'Belhaven' Miss Norris understood, for the smell was there, the same smell, everywhere, male, disgusting, signal of fear.

The house was very quiet. Maisie was sitting on the floor of her room, which was unlocked, looking at her picture books. When she saw the rage in her sister's face she pushed the books away and scrambled to her feet.

"You let them in!" Mary accused her in a terrible voice.

"I never."

"You must have. Your door is unlocked. How else did they get in?"

"They had the keys."

"That's a lie. How could they have my keys?"

"Not a lie. They had the keys. They found them. They did. They did!"

Miss Norris rushed down to her desk. The truth lay there waiting for her. The spare front door key was not in the right-hand drawer where she always kept it, but amongst the jumble of old stuff in the left-hand one. And that of her room?

Back upstairs she held out her hand.

"Give me the spare key of your room! Quick!"

Maisie, now terrified, bustled over to her toy cupboard and fishing it out, handed it over, beginning to cry miserably.

"You wicked, wicked girl!" Mary panted. She was terrified herself. It was a betrayal! Unlooked for, unimaginable treachery! Her slave, her tool, her willing, stupid, loathed, useless, usefully trained —

"No!" Maisie shrieked, as her sister, who had rushed from the room came back with the instruments of punishment. "No. Good girl! Maisie good! Good! NO! No!"

"Yes, yes," Miss Norris grated in the voice and manner that had always paralysed the mind and body of her life-long victim.

The heavily tiled and double-glazed bathroom deadened the screams before they were effectively silenced; the bath was there to wash away the blood.

17

When Detective Inspector Holmes called at 'Belhaven' on the day after Farrer and Goff had seen Maisie there, Miss Mary Norris had at first fallen into a rage that rendered her nearly speechless. This was succeeded, as she opened the door to him, by equally paralysing fear. But when he walked in and stood in the hall and asked gravely for her sister, she realised, with mounting relief, followed at once by hope, that here lay a possible escape for herself and a permanent solution of her domestic problem.

"You want to see Maisie?"

She decided it would be best if she did not mention the other two officers' visit to the house the day before.

"Yes, Miss Norris. I would like you and your sister to come with me for another interview with the Detective Superintendent."

"*Another?*"

"It would help us very materially in our inquiries into the death of Sister Hallet at St. Edmunds Hospital."

Miss Norris put on a very serious face indeed.

"Maisie is not very well this morning. I'm afraid she

had an upsetting experience yesterday afternoon. She was alone in the house. She is not used to strangers forcing their way in," she finished on a vicious note.

"I'm afraid you exaggerate," Holmes said stiffly. "I am asking you now if you would kindly assist us further by bringing your sister, in my car, for a fresh interview. Certainly she will not be alone, for you will be with her."

"Very well," Miss Norris agreed, holding the worried look. "You make me very anxious — very anxious indeed. Poor Maisie. She has never been answerable for her actions."

Detective Inspector Holmes thanked her and suggested she might bring her sister down from upstairs at once.

"And I would like you to bring your V.A.D. overalls with you," he added. "You need not put them on, just bring them."

"My uniform?" Miss Norris was genuinely confused.

"The overall you wore for work in the wards. You have two, I understand. I would like you to bring both."

Again fear swept Miss Norris, confusing, choking fear. But she turned and went away without another word. Holmes sat down on the single chair in the hall, beside the telephone. But he spoke a few words into the two-way radio he carried.

Presently the sisters walked slowly down the stairs, side by side, Mary holding Maisie firmly by the hand. Inspector Holmes greeted the latter but she did not answer, nor even look at him, but only at her sister, whose hand she continued to hold.

When they reached the car, the woman police driver, in uniform, got out to open the rear door for them and when Maisie hung back with a little grunting cry, urged her forward kindly. Maisie then dropped Mary's hand, climbed in and settled herself in one corner, rubbing the hand she had recovered as if Mary's hold had squeezed it into numbness. They drove off.

Nothing had been said about their destination, which was St. Edmunds Hospital. Miss Norris had guessed it correctly and was prepared. Maisie was not. When the car stopped at the main entrance she began to babble, using short, rapid phrases of dislike and reluctance, repeated again and again. But the police woman soothed and reassured her, while her sister got out of the car in silence to stand beside the Detective Inspector, watching, wholly withdrawn, with the working overalls in a plastic bag dangling from one hand and her black handbag from the other. When the three were together on the steps the policewoman drove the car away.

Joe Wells watched the scene from his lodge but did not come out. There had already been several interesting arrivals. Something was up. The cops — he was too old to feel anything but downright silly if he called them 'pigs' — the cops were fixing something in Hunter Ward. Barmy, really. The ward had been totally empty with Fred Gates moved to the chest hospital and young Lionel well enough again to go home. Looked like staying empty now that agency nurses were being got rid of as well as paying patients. Not exactly what they'd wanted, that.

So Wells ignored the fresh arrivals and they went up in the lift with Armstrong, whose dark eyes rolled in their sockets at the sight of the two Miss Norrises, close together for once. He'd been aware of them, much alike, but separate, in the days of crisis, now happily over. It gave him a queer feeling to see them together.

The lift arrived at Hunter Ward and there were Detective Superintendent Farrer and Detective Sergeant Goff waiting to receive them. The two women stepped out, Holmes stepped back. At a word from him Armstrong closed the lift doors and pressed the button to descend.

The Norris sisters stood still, quite silent too, making no response to the policemen's polite greetings. Then Sister Baker stepped from behind the two men and said to Miss Norris, "I see you have brought your overall. And your sister's too."

"They are both mine," said Miss Norris quickly.

"Well, never mind. Your sister always wore one when she came to help us. Didn't you?" Sister asked, turning suddenly to face Maisie, who had lagged a little behind Mary, as they moved out of the lift.

"Yes, I did," Maisie said boldly. Mary thrust out a menacing arm, but the other shrank out of range.

"Never mind," Sister went on, placing herself now between the two. Being taller than either it seemed natural for her to put a hand to the shoulder of each sister to urge them gently forward.

"We would like you both to take off your coats and put on your overalls," she added. "I'm sure you remember where you used to put them when you were helping us. Well, it was in here, wasn't it?" She opened the door opposite her office. "And I'm sure you remember Nurse Shaw and Nurse Street."

Maisie hesitated, went forward, looked back at Mary and held out a hand for an overall. With a half-angry, half-laughing and wholly contemptuous exclamation, Miss Norris plucked one garment from the bag she carried and tossed it forward. Then turned.

"What is this silly farce in aid of?" she asked. "Those two solemn idiots at the lift who have been pestering me with questions, and all this palaver with the V.A.D. uniform. What's it in aid of, may I ask?"

"No good asking me" Sister Baker said. "I'm just doing what Mr. Farrer suggested. May I help you?"

She was speaking to Maisie, who accepted her aid, while Patty came forward to hold the overall for her and Tim did rather more than ease Miss Norris out of the coat she had reluctantly unbuttoned.

Meanwhile, in Sister's room Detective Superintendent Farrer was explaining matters to Mrs. Mitchell, Mrs. Gates, Nurse Biggs, the registrars and the consultants and the Sister from Ward VI, whose name was Moon.

"I have asked you all to come here because we need your help over identification," he said. "We have a complete list of the hours of work put in by the various V.A.D.s during the emergency and where they did them. Their officially recognised hours, that is. But the Miss Norrises were seen, one or other of them, at other times. Always either in Hunter Ward here, or on their way up or down the stairs from the third floor and Ward VI."

"I must say I never saw more than one, the same one," Sister Moon said firmly.

"I'm sure I saw both and confused them, one with another," Sister Baker declared. "And so did my nurses."

Nurse Biggs nodded. "I didn't realise there were two. But then my sightings or hearings were brief and in most disturbing circumstances."

"You were on night duty, weren't you?"

"I was. I couldn't have told them apart in the semi-dark."

"Fred did," Mrs. Gates put in suddenly. "But then we'd known them for years, as children, Maisie, poor mite, wanting from birth, she was, and Mary, the mother spoilt her till Maisie was born and then gave it all to Maisie."

Farrer let Mrs. Gates run on. He wanted the others to understand that sinister domestic situation compounded of jealousy, hatred, limited understanding, retarded mental powers, with over all a total parental indifference from a father who had never wanted to have children at all.

"The mother seems to have been in poor health for many years," Farrer said, when Mrs. Gates showed signs of drying up.

"I suppose some of it was genuine," Mrs. Gates said. "I know she was scared of that Mary. Too scared to stop her venting her spite on the poor little creature. Treated her like a dog, she did. Mary, I mean. Literally. She didn't walk till she was nearly five, Maisie didn't. So then to stop her wandering and getting run over, they always said, they let Mary put the dog's collar on her, not a proper child's harness, and take her about the garden in it. Lashed her with the lead, too."

There were exclamations of horror from the women and grunts of disgust from the doctors. Mrs. Gates was encouraged to develop the drama.

"It came to a head when the Health Visitor called unexpected. There were only two in our district, Visitors, I mean, and a Medical Officer of Health, who knew every case on the books. Now it's all committees and that, no one really responsible, Fred says, nothing done, all talk and paper. You know what I mean, Sister, don't you? They had a case —"

Farrer recalled Mrs. Gates to the matter in hand.

"Mr. Gates in his deposition says it was owing to the scandal in that neighbourhood that the Norrises moved right away to the house where the two sisters now live in Priory Road."

"That's right. Took the dog with them. I expect it died before long."

There was a knock on the door. Detective Sergeant Goff was standing outside, the two sisters behind him, Patty and Tim across the corridor, watching.

The door opened, Goff stood back, the sisters went in.

In a low voice Patty said, "You're not on your own now, are you?"

"I'm not here at all." Tim answered. "I'm in Out-patients. This ward's been closed since Monday."

"But you weren't on your own?"

"Of course not. We had Chu Ling. Malay. Fantastic. No English, but that's immaterial."

"I bet. Where's she gone now?"

"Out-patients."

"You're in luck, then?"

"Management, sweetie."

They turned back into the kitchen.

"Sister did say we'd better lay on tea for afterwards," Tim said. "I'll put on a kettle anyway."

"After what?"

"This meeting or confrontation or whatever it is. To prove the barmy one knocked off old Hallet."

"*If!* But she certainly did have a go at Mr. Gates and at me. I hope they put her away. Rampton, isn't it?"

"For men, yes. I don't know about women."

The Norris sisters, (as they had been known in Priory Road for so many years and were now to be known as such throughout the country) moved slowly into Sister Baker's room, Maisie, as usual, a little behind Mary. As it was such a small room, with so many people in it, they had to stop just inside the door, leaving Sergeant Goff outside.

In their identical white hospital overalls, they appeared very much more alike than in their outdoor coats, their dark skirts and jumpers. If Maisie's figure was more lumpy, more ungainly than Mary's, her arms were a trifle longer, her hands broader and stronger. Her neck and the lower part of her face seemed to be thicker than her sister's, but the noses were identical, the foreheads equally low, the greying hair as straight and sparse. Only the eyes were markedly different, though of similar size; Mary's being bright, defiant, filling with angry sparks as they swept the company before her, while Maisie's, under swollen lids, began to fill with tears.

Mrs. Mitchell broke the silence.

"I told you," she said, speaking to Detective Superintendent Farrer, "I told you she had watery eyes. Look at her!"

They all looked; it was obvious which Miss Norris she meant. Maisie shrank back against the door.

"That's our Maisie all right," Mrs. Gates agreed. "I'd know her anywhere. Fred was dead right."

Nurse Biggs nodded. The doctors gave no sign. The two Sisters exchanged glances. Sister Moon said firmly, "I'm quite sure that one was never in my ward. The other was, at the times you have on your list."

"I think they both came to Hunter," Sister Baker said. "I'm afraid I didn't realise there were two of them. I feel sure Miss Mary was here the first day the V.A.D.s came to help. She was here the next day when Sister Hallet came back from the theatre. That was in the morning. I was off duty that night, of course."

"When it seems certain that one of these sisters was heard to be in cubicle 1, attending to Sister Hallet and in cubicle 2 with Miss Parker."

Farrer paused and Miss Norris, turning to the shrinking, terrified Maisie said in a sorrowful voice. "Oh, Maisie, what have you done? What have you done?"

Maisie began to sob, began to babble, "Not bad! Good girl! Not bad!"

Miss Norris turned a grief-stricken face to the company. "She always wanted to copy me," she explained. "She often used to put on my second overall, though I had to keep all the clothes we possessed in my room because she has these destructive urges. So when the call came for emergency help she must have followed my example and come to the hospital."

"She was never noticed entering by the front hall," said Farrer. "How did she get in?"

"I suppose by the fire-escape," said Miss Norris. "It was kept closed but unlocked, I believe, during the emergency."

Sister Baker nodded.

"You suppose then that she came up the fire-escape, perhaps to find you, wearing the overall. She was given a few jobs by Sister. She stayed on — where?"

"Where?" Miss Norris looked affronted. "How do I know where? The hospital was in a state of chaos, wasn't it? She could have wandered around, unnoticed."

"At night?"

"Well, at night she could have hidden, couldn't she? There was one empty cubicle up here, wasn't there? I was told that the first day I worked here."

"Yes." Farrer's voice took on a severer note. "Yes, Miss Norris, you learned several things that first morning. Maisie was not with you that time. You learned that Miss Hallet, whom you considered your arch enemy was in cubicle 1, very ill. You saw how easy it would be to hide in cubicle 8 just opposite. You learned that the fire-escape was in frequent use."

"I don't see what you are driving at?" exclaimed Miss Norris, whose temper was slipping fast. "Poor Maisie can't understand all this. How can she know the dreadful things —"

"You ordered her to do and saw that she did them."

"*I!*"

"Yes, Miss Norris, *you*. How could Maisie leave your house without your connivance? You kept her locked in when you went out, always locked in."

"She had a second key," panted Miss Norris.

"You did not know that until after she had let me in with it this week."

"She must have come up the fire-escape! She must!"

"Directed by you and told what she was to do. Directed by you while you attacked Nurse Biggs in the grounds, after the attempt to silence Mr. Gates earlier that week had failed."

"Is it likely?" Miss Norris shouted her denial. "Is it likely I would tell her, or in some way make her go for the nurses here with a knife she must have picked up in the kitchen."

"On her own, no," Farrer answered, as calmly as ever. "But all these events have two aspects; one of wicked scheming and one of senseless rage. It was not until I understood this dual nature of the crimes that I knew two different hands had been at work. Yours, Miss Norris, that of the leader, Maisie's the tool."

"Prove it!" Miss Norris cried. "Prove it! You never will!"

At this moment Maisie, who could bear no more of a quarrel she did not at all understand, but which she felt her sister was not going to win, backed to the door, turned, tore it open, rushed past Detective Sergeant Goff into the kitchen opposite, seized the bread knife from the table where Tim had just laid it, and dashed back across the corridor.

"I told you!" shrieked Miss Norris, taking cover behind the Detective Superintendent, for there was no mistaking the object of Maisie's rage and hate. "I told you. Stop her! Murderess! Murderess!"

Maisie flung the knife, pretty hard and straight, but Farrer dodged it, pushing Miss Norris aside at the same time. Maisie turned and ran.

Her terror grew. In place of the narrow corridor with the enclosing curtains, the ward was an open space, a confusion of empty beds and metal frames, bright metal catching the sun from one long line of windows; shining back at her, muddling still more her feeble wits, but drowning her rage in an overwhelming desire to get away at last from Mary. Her understanding was not so poor that she did not know her sister was herself in great trouble and great fear, that the power she wielded had met a greater power. This too she must escape and her determination kept her terror down, so that she did not lose her way in the bewildering emptiness of the ward, but kept straight on to the bathroom, the landing, the door of the fire-escape.

Detective Sergeant Goff, the first to arrive in pursuit, saw her fumbling with the fire-escape door. It only needed the routine method of opening, and the directions were printed in large type and simple words above, but Maisie could not do it, had never been capable of doing it. Mary had always opened the door for her and now she was helpless, trapped.

Shouts and the sound of running feet came from behind them.

Maisie turned an anguished, frantic face to Goff.

"Please!" she panted. "Open it, *please*!"

Against reason, but with the thought of his own small girl clear in his sentimental mind at that moment,

Goff opened the door wide. In a second Maisie was through and had launched herself upon the rail of the escape.

The pursuers gathered to watch. Firmly held on either side by the two policemen, Miss Norris watched her little sister slide from her power for ever. At every turn Maisie landed with perfect precision and launched herself again. The steep incline, greater than in any normal house stairs, increased her speed. She slipped away incredibly fast, floating, it seemed, without effort, until she landed on the ground, still neatly controlled, but wringing her hands that had suffered from the harsh rusted paint on the rail.

Detective Inspector Holmes, who had stood at the foot of the escape watching the descent, stepped forward.

"Take me home, please," Maisie said, dragging off the ruined overall and pulling down her skirt.

"Yes, miss," said Holmes, "I'll take you in my car. You did that very well, if I may say so."

She looked up at him, tears now filling the weak eyes and beginning to fall down the heavy cheeks.

18

COUNSEL FOR THE prosecution, summing up, said "You have heard evidence proving that Sister Hallet's death was brought about by the administration of a gross overdose of pain-killing narcotic. You have heard how the excessive dose in three pre-sterilised hypodermic syringes was made available. You can have no doubt that the drug so given was deliberately designed to kill. Motive was there, the means, the opportunity. Your only doubt may lie in two questions, the answer to one being in favour of the prisoner's innocence, the other answer against. How could a subnormal, mentally retarded woman administer the drug? And how could such a person plan such a murder? For murder it was, members of the jury. You can have no doubt of that.

"You must therefore consider what we know from the evidence of the strange actions that can only be attributed to the handicapped being, Maisie Norris, who was not before you in the dock, being found unfit to plead. But it has been shown that she must have given the so-called 'dirty injection' in the arm, causing an abscess, to Miss Daphne Parker. Was this childish malice or was it an action conceived in her muddled mind to compensate for the dose no longer available for post-operative treatment because it had gone into Sister Hallet? It is not likely it was authorised by the cunning mind that devised the murder, for it was one of the most telling and foreseeable clues, later revealed, in the exposure of the whole strange and horrible plot. It was a fatal mistake, if mistake it was, on the part of the real murderer. You have been told of the stupidity, the crudeness of the later assaults. Clearly Maisie's work. But why was she in Hunter Ward at night? Because Mary opened the fire-escape door for her. She could not do that herself.

"So we come to the nature and working of the hideous control the prisoner exercised over her afflicted sister."

Here Counsel repeated the evidence of Health Visitors, local Councils and selected neighbours, including Mrs. Gates, to prove the facts of Maisie's mental deficiency, her upbringing and her sister's growing ascendance. He continued, "We cannot dispute that Mary Norris looked after her sister in all material ways. She fed and clothed her, she called a doctor if Maisie was ill. But she kept her a close prisoner in the house and garden; she never allowed her to go out alone, even in the charge of a neighbour. And as time went on and there was no halt in the developing sadism Mary exhibited in her control over her helpless victim; the physical expression of it became an obscene horror. As a punishment frequently applied, you have heard how the victim was rendered helpless with leather straps about her arms and legs. A dog collar, a larger version of that belonging to a former family pet, was fastened about her neck, so tight that her screams were stifled by near strangling, and then she was lashed unmercifully with a leather dog lead on the back, buttocks and thighs. You have heard that the scars upon the victim's body show clearly the appalling record of these assaults. Can you question Maisie's obedience to her sister's orders? Can you do other than find Mary Norris guilty, as prime mover and chief accessory, the brain, the will, the director of deliberate murder, the prime mover, also, of those assaults upon possible witnesses of her crime."

Counsel for the defence made the most of Maisie's more lurid, more normal moments. She was not as handicapped mentally as she had been painted. Sympathy for her genuine sufferings had blinded people to the fact of her real, ungovernable, irrational and violent temper. She had been the prime mover, not the willing instrument of her sister. She was not entirely under Mary's control. He pointed out her behaviour in opening the door of 'Belhaven' to the police detectives. Also her marked athletic ability in her final escape and the favourable, but guarded, report from the Warden of the Home for Mentally Disturbed Women, where she was now living.

The jury, after many hours, was not able to reach a unanimous, or even a majority verdict as to the charge of murder. Because clearly Mary had not actually done the killing. They sought further direction from the judge. They sought permission to find a verdict of manslaughter through the misapplied actions of Maisie, who had not been allowed to plead. But they considered both sisters were guilty of criminal assault, Mary upon her sister and Maisie upon the other victims in Hunter Ward.

Eventually, however, the jury agreed upon a verdict

of guilty of murder. Mary was sentenced to life imprisonment. She continued to declare her innocence and filed an appeal.

Dr. Fisher and Dr. Thompson were enjoying their honeymoon in Italy when David managed to find a slightly out-dated copy of *The Times.* In it was a full account of the death in her prison cell of the notorious criminal, Mary Norris.

"Strangled, it says," David exclaimed.

"Let me see. Oh, *no*!"

"What –?"

"A dog collar," Joan read aloud, "was fastened tightly round her neck, choking her. There were no other signs of violence —"

"Let me see!" David read on. "The collar belonged to a labrador owned by one of the prison guards employed in the grounds. It is not known how or by whom the collar was brought into the prison."

"Nor who used it, I suppose?" said Joan, shuddering.

"Retribution by fellow prisoners, perhaps. She had asked to stay in her cell, she was so unpopular, I was told."

"Some prisoners work in the gardens and chicken houses. They could meet the labrador out of doors."

"Or she could have done it herself. That can happen. One of the forensic chaps says so. He listed several cases of self-strangulation."

"Then she was as cracked as poor Maisie, wasn't she?" He threw the newspaper away.

"Does that matter? Does it alter anything? The evil was done, all the evil. We were —"

"*Not guilty*!" said Joan, firmly, reaching for his hand. "So take that doom-look off your face, my darling!"